The Heir

John Hagen

Dedication

To my wife, Ileana who is my constant source of joy and happiness.

Acknowledgment

This novel is a work of fiction. Although, I have travelled and performed surgery in other countries, any resemblance to actual events is coincidence. Everest base camp captured my imagination, and this was the origin of my motivation to write this novel. I would like to thank my wife, Ileana and Mattan, who accompanied me on the trip to Mt. Everest.

Thank you to Janet Gyenes, who helped with the editing. Any mistakes in the text, however, are mine. Thank you to KDP publishing with the promotion and publishing of the novel.

Contents

Page Blank Intentionally

About The Author

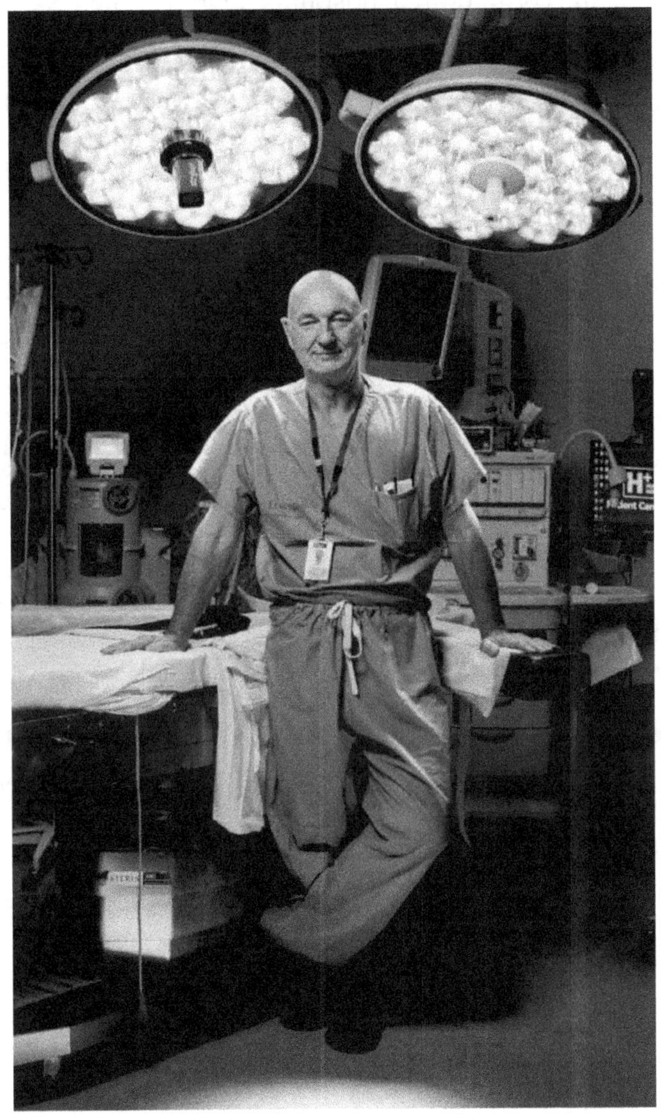

Dr. John Hagen completed his doctor of medicine (honours) degree from the University of Alberta in 1979, later attaining specialty training in areas such as endoscopy. He's spent much of his practice in Toronto-area hospitals in roles such as attending surgeon, division head of general surgery, surgical director of bariatrics, and chief of surgery, among others. Now retired from practice, Hagen has taken on several instructor responsibilities: he currently holds a trio of roles as supervising surgeon and instructor at the University of Toronto Surgery Training Program, and has won several teaching awards for his work. Since 2005, Hagen has lectured widely and delivered myriad courses and live demonstrations, particularly in laparoscopic and bariatric surgery, in Canada, the US, UK, Europe, Mexico, Nepal, Colombia and China.

The Heir is Hagen's sixth novel, following five other medical thrillers, *The Clinic*, 2024, *The Embryo* (2023), *The Mission* (2024), *The Complication* (2024) and *The Sailor* (2023). Along with being a dedicated lecturer and volunteer at medical missions with his wife, Ileana, the couple are avid travellers and sailors. They live in King City, Ontario, and spend time taking excursions on their 51-foot sailboat, *Ileana,* having sailed to the Caribbean and the Bahamas for the winter months.

Preface

It was one of those soul-crushing headaches that pounded relentlessly. A wave of complete incapacity washed over him. He felt a sharp, splitting sensation at the front of his head, as if a wedge was prying it away from the rest of his skull. A neoprene face guard concealed his appearance, leaving only his mouth and eyes visible to the outside world. The wind howled around him, whipping the snow through the air in a frenzy of horizontal streaks. Then it got worse. An avalanche unleashed its fury on the mountain, catching him off guard and burying him beneath the weight of the snow. In the pitch-black surroundings, he could hear nothing but his own heartbeat, intensifying his sense of isolation. At 17,598 feet, the air was so thin that each breath was a desperate battle for survival, heightening his feeling of imminent disaster. If he had any hope of getting off the mountain alive, he had to find a way to calm down.

Chapter One

John Hegland was down to the last few hundred metres of his run through his neighbourhood in Toronto. Running 10 kilometres every day helped keep him sane. At just 39, he shouldered the huge responsibility of being chief of staff at his hospital while still juggling a full surgical practice, stressful roles that required him to maintain a high level of both physical and mental fitness. His brow glistened with sweat and his trendy seven-day-old beard felt oppressive in the warm spring sun. His singlet clung to his chest, damp with perspiration. John approached his home with a last burst of energy. The problems of today faded away, leaving his mind clear.

"Hi honey," he said to his partner, Suzie, when he walked into the kitchen. She'd had her head in her hands and looked up from the table where she sat. Still catching his breath, John stopped in his tracks. "What's wrong?"

Her shoulder-length hair, a beautiful mane of thick, black curls, framed her face. The corners of her mouth were turned into a pout. Yet somehow that seemed to highlight her flawless olive complexion, a testament to Suzie's Colombian heritage. Standing on her toes, she pressed her lips against his, avoiding any contact with his damp body. Suzie sniffed at his sweaty body and smiled. "You are so much better after your run." Sitting back down in her chair, she said, "I'm a little stressed. I saw five new patients today. The psychological toll on these kids was a little overwhelming."

"Do you miss the classroom?" asked John. "You were so good at teaching. All the kids loved you."

Suzie sighed and rolled her eyes. They had talked about this before, and John knew the idea of her quitting her job as a teacher was a significant step. Transitioning from teaching to establishing a solo psychology practice for troubled children was a financial gamble.

"Yeah, I miss the kids, but psychology has always been my passion. I still see some of the kids, but our interactions have become more personal and focused on one child at a time." She looked up at John and smiled. "Having some control over my life is a tremendous advantage. You know that's it has always bothered me that the control over teachers by the unions and school boards stifles individual thought. So much for independent decision-making."

"I'm not trying to tell you what to do," said John, his voice softening. "I'm just a little worried; you're already booking appointments three weeks away. As time goes on, you will become increasingly busy." He paused and kissed Suzie on the top of her head. "You had the courage to venture out on your own. Not sure how you could leave the cushy elementary school job to do this. Good for you, though. There are so many kids who are suffering, and they need your help."

Suzie smiled. John had made it abundantly clear to her he fully supported her transition, offering unwavering encouragement. As much as he tried, he'd been unable to hide his uncertainty about her potential to earn a living from it. Not only had she been responsible for educating Grade 6 students, but she'd also taken on the role of school psychologist for the past six years. Psychotherapy was the aspect of her job that she found most satisfying, and what she talked about with John after work.

He knew she was very good at it, too. By observing the movement of the child's body and closely watching their eyes, she possessed the ability to identify the source of their problem with a high degree of accuracy. She told John that if a child's eyes looked up and to the left, they were likely lying. Coupled with the fidgeting of the hands and restlessness of the legs, it became a certainty. Suzie pointed out whenever she noticed the children could not meet her gaze directly and maintain eye contact, she knew they were concealing something. When she asked the child to look her directly in the eyes, it was common for them to reveal their unsettling secret.

Over the two and a half years they had been living together, sometimes it was almost as if she could also read his mind, too. From the moment he walked into the house, she could pinpoint whether something was bothering him. Earlier today had been an example of her extraordinary abilities. He had met with a surgeon for the last few weeks to discuss the doctor's problem with alcohol consumption. Today, when John suggested he seek treatment, the surgeon went into a rage, threatening legal action before he stormed out of John's office. Even though John knew he had to confront the surgeon, anxiety coursed through John's body and his pulse raced from the interaction.

"On the drive home, I tried to think of my next step, but nothing came to me," he explained to Suzie when he arrived home from work. Without looking up from where she was sitting at the kitchen table, Suzie said, "You have anxiety. You need to go for a run and then we'll talk."

Suzie told John that people with anxiety emit pheromones that have a noticeable scent resembling wet paper. She explained that animals easily reacted to these pheromones, which was why a dog might become aggressive towards someone who feared them, while gladly seeking belly rubs from someone who didn't. Her ability to detect anxiety coming from parents and children was helpful in Suzie's psychotherapy practice.

The one detrimental effect of detecting these pheromones was that it made her angry, just like the dogs who encountered these pheromones from people. Over time, she became adept at controlling her anger by acknowledging and understanding the emotion. Before speaking, she would silently count to 10, using this psychological trick to compose herself and avoid making any untoward remarks to the parents or students that could heighten their anxiety.

After coming back from his run, John could feel his anxiety and stress had dissipated. He could now have a conversation with Suzie without worrying about her getting angry. Suzie's ability to read people was a gift that frequently prevented John from getting into trouble. He'd invite Suzie to accompany him to meet a new financial advisor, or investment counsellor, for example, seeking her perspective on whether they could trust them. Her assessments were seldom inaccurate, demonstrating her keen judgment.

John sat down at the table. "Hey, no pressure. But have you decided whether you can come to Kathmandu with me for the medical conference? a way," he said.

The prospect of speaking at an international meeting in Kathmandu provided a much-needed respite from the long, demanding days at the hospital. John specialized in bariatric surgery, a procedure specifically designed to address obesity. Recognized for his expertise in the field, he was scheduled to give a comprehensive presentation to an esteemed panel of international experts. The topic of his talk revolved around the remarkable effects of obesity surgery in treating infertility among patients diagnosed with polycystic ovarian syndrome, delving into the scientific evidence and case studies.

Although the opportunity to speak at such a prestigious meeting was flattering, the offer to take him and Suzie to Mount Everest Base Camp by helicopter was even more enticing. It would be in early May, the beginning of the climbing season. John wanted to revel in the sense of anticipation and excitement being around elite mountaineers, risking everything to conquer the mountain, even though he wasn't a climber himself. Over the years they had been together, Suzie had counselled John on his fear of heights. He knew it was so overwhelming that he could never entertain the idea of scaling a rock face and staring down into the abyss. Nevertheless, the allure of others conquering one of the most majestic and treacherous wonders of nature captivated his imagination.

Suzie turned her gaze towards John. A smile lit up her face. "There's absolutely no way I would miss this adventure for anything in the world."

Chapter Two

Travelling in business class made the otherwise gruelling 12-hour flight from Toronto to New Delhi much more tolerable. John took full advantage of the seats that could flatten, and he slept for most of the journey. After a weekend of being on call at the hospital, he was sleep deprived. Although there were surgical residents who helped to look after the admitted patients, the emergency room had been exceptionally busy. John had spent the last two nights operating in the early hours of the morning.

The last patient had a perforated colon from diverticulitis. He was hypotensive from sepsis, but his condition stabilized after John removed the infected colon and created a colostomy. The patient remained in the ICU, relying on vasopressors to maintain adequate blood pressure and perfuse the vital organs. The doctor in the intensive care unit had informed the family that the chances of survival were approximately fifty-fifty. Because of his own personal duty, John was reluctant to leave a sick patient in the care of others. However, he also had a commitment to speak at the meeting, so he could not delay the trip. The privilege of working with a highly supportive group of colleagues who were more than willing to take over allowed for a seamless transfer of patient care.

While waiting for their connecting flight to Kathmandu, Suzie and John opted for the comfortable Air India business lounge during their two-hour layover at the New Delhi airport.

"I have a hard time sleeping on the plane," said Suzie. "Why is it every time I walked by to say hi, you were peacefully snoozing, completely out of it? Do you really want me to be part of this trip or are you going to continue to ignore me?" she teased.

"It's not my fault the brutal call of the past two nights had exhausted me," said John. "I feel like I have finally caught up on my sleep. Now I feel refreshed and rejuvenated." He leaned over the coffee table and kissed her lips. "Of course I want you to be part of this adventure." Her frown and furrowed brow changed instantly into a bright smile.

Suzie's tone softened. "You are a good sleeper," she quipped. "You can probably sleep standing up. Have you ever fallen over while asleep in the operating room?"

"Very funny," laughed John. "I can fall asleep in 10 seconds. My surgical training taught me how to do that. Standing up and falling asleep, though, was not part of the curriculum."

John was drinking espresso and Suzie a glass of white wine. "One of us has not adjusted to the time change," said Suzie. "Kathmandu is 10:45 hours ahead of us in Toronto, so according to me, it is after 5 p.m., just in time for my evening glass of wine."

"I wonder why the time is 45 minutes out?" John said. "I

thought that only happened in Newfoundland and Labrador, since they are half an hour later than us."

"Probably for the same reason. Without fail, Newfoundlanders are always running behind schedule for appointments by approximately thirty minutes."

"Ha ha," laughed John. "You need to get some rest!" He paused as he listened to the overhead announcement. "They are calling for our flight. We better get moving."

John and Suzie finished their drinks and headed for the departure gate. The group of people gathered around was distinct from the individuals who were on the flight to New Delhi. These travellers were relatively young, probably between 20 and 45. Most appeared to be slender and fit. The air buzzed with people speaking Dutch, German, Norwegian, and Spanish. John looked around the terminal and his eyes met the gaze of a man sitting on a chair who seemed to be around the same age. There was a fleeting moment of recognition in John's mind as made his way towards the man.

"Eduardo?" John asked. Despite the man's older age and casual attire of brown cargo pants, a blue Mountain Gear T-shirt and bare feet in sandals, John would recognize those piercing eyes and chiselled facial features anywhere. "Eduardo," he said, disbelievingly, trying to remember the man's last name. "Eduardo… Rattazzi. Is that you?"

The man seemed to unfold his thin build as he stood up, his height commanding attention. He ran a hand through his shoulder-length curly hair. The jet-black locks shone in the harsh light of the airport. After a moment, his eyes softened with recognition. "I don't believe it. John Hegland. What? It's been… 20 years. What the devil are you doing here?"

"I'm on my way to Kathmandu to give some talks at an international surgery meeting," he replied. "What are you doing here?"

There was a momentary pause of silence from Eduardo. "I'm on my way to climb Mount Everest."

John looked at Eduardo incredulously. He still wasn't convinced this could be the same Eduardo he knew from school in South Wales. It had been 20 years, and everything about him had changed. The Eduardo he remembered was interested in the dramatic arts and fashion. He was the best dressed student at the school. No one else had as many pairs of shoes in their closet; his collection surpassed theirs combined. Eduardo's closets were full of colourful clothes, and he'd wear a different outfit every day. Despite the school's offering of unique activities like kayaking, cliff-rescue training, and beach-rescue training, Eduardo had shown absolutely no interest in any outdoor sports except for sailing. His exceptional good looks captivated women, yet he displayed no interest in their advances. John later realized Eduardo was gay, but that didn't change their friendship. In fact, in some ways, it was even more special since Eduardo trusted John and appreciated his open-mindedness.

Suzie smoothly slid up next to John, her presence going unnoticed by Eduardo, who was talking about his itinerary. "Honey," said John when he felt her arm on his back, "I'd like you to meet Eduardo. We went to school together 20 years ago. He just told me he plans to climb Mount Everest."

"A pleasure to meet you," said Eduardo as he shook Suzie's hand.

"You too," said Suzie. "We had better get on board. We are the last ones."

The three of them climbed up the steps and entered the plane, greeted by the scent of jet fuel. Since the flight was not full, Eduardo found an empty seat next to John.

"I'm going to have a nap," announced Suzie as she leaned her head against the window, using the supplied pillow as a cushion. As the plane taxied down the runway, she was already fast asleep, softly snoring.

"Forgive me for being presumptuous, Eduardo," John said, his eyebrows raised in disbelief, "but you, of all people, climbing

Mount Everest is quite unexpected."

Eduardo turned slightly to look at John. "It was not something I expected from myself either." His voice was full of surprise. "Two weeks ago, I stood atop Annapurna, taking in the breathtaking view of the surrounding Himalayan peaks. Annapurna is 500 metres less than Everest, but still over 8,000 metres. My team of sherpas and guides are meeting me at the base camp tomorrow. Usually, an Everest expedition takes eight weeks to acclimatize, but having recently scaled Annapurna, I'm ready. Over the next week, they will take me to Everest Base Camp 2 and then to Camp 3 to further prepare for the summit."

John was astonished. "What happened to you?" he asked. "I remember you getting in trouble for refusing to partake in the ritual morning swim at school. Yet here you are risking your life on the deadliest of mountains on Earth."

Eduardo fell silent once more, the weight of his thoughts palpable to John. "Life has not always brought me happiness and relevance. It is difficult for many to understand, given my privileged background. Until a few months ago, it had been over 10 years since I last had a conversation with my father. He is still the richest man in Italy. He expected me to take over the business, but I knew early on he would never allow that. After leaving Princeton, I spent the first decade wandering around the globe, trying to come to a better understanding of what life was all about. I switched religions to become a Muslim, hoping to find answers, but quickly became disillusioned. Now I'm finding solace in re-reading the Quran. After I railed about the evils of capitalism all over social media and in the Italian press, my father disowned me."

John listened intently. When Eduardo paused, he said, "About 10 years ago, I read in the international news that you were arrested in Kenya for possession of heroin. That must have been a rough time for you."

"I got acquitted, thanks to my father's influence, but 13 of my friends are still in jail over there." Eduardo shook his head, thinking about the memory. Then he spilled his guts. It was as if 20 years had melted, and the two men were confidantes again. "Despite having stayed at the most expensive rehabilitation clinics on the planet, I still struggle with addiction to heroin." Eduardo looked down and lowered his voice. "I had a relapse six months ago."

John's eyes widened, but he didn't want to interrupt his old friend.

"One client at my last rehab clinic was a mountaineer, and we became friends. He convinced me to give high-altitude climbing a chance. Besides, he would say, 'What is the worst that could happen? You could die on the mountain and your misery would come to an end.'"

"Eduardo, I knew none of this," said John. "The moment we stepped out of the school premises all those years ago, it seemed as if we were exiting a realm of make-believe, leaving us ill-equipped to navigate the practicalities of the real world. Many of us had difficulties adjusting, but you have had the toughest road to travel. I have always known there is something special about you that perhaps you have yet to realize. Many acknowledge that climbing mountains is undoubtedly one of the most physically and mentally demanding experiences one can undertake on this planet, and yet your nonchalant attitude towards it truly amazes me. If I had successfully climbed Annapurna, every social media platform and news outlet would broadcast my achievement for everyone to hear."

Eduardo smiled at John. "Despite enduring and emerging stronger from the experience, I still find myself feeling no more satisfied with my achievements. Look at you. A famous surgeon giving talks around the world. That must be immensely satisfying, spending your life helping others. If only I possessed the same level of constitution, purpose in life, and accompanying happiness resulting from relevance that you do, I would consider myself truly blessed."

Their conversation halted as the announcement played through the airplane's speakers. In 20 minutes, they would touch down in Kathmandu. The seatbelt light flashed on. John and Eduardo exchanged phone numbers and emails. They both promised to stay in touch using WhatsApp. The moment the plane's wheels touched the tarmac, the jarring impact abruptly interrupted Suzie's peaceful slumber. Minutes later, they got up from their seats. Both Suzie and John hugged Eduardo goodbye, wishing him the best of luck in his attempt to summit Everest.

Suzie watched as Eduardo exited the plane. She turned to John and whispered, "My senses are on high alert with that fellow, John. He's in a lot of trouble."

Chapter Three

The icy April wind blew in from the Atlantic almost directly at them. The two 17-year-olds were sailing through the enormous waves of the Bristol Channel, South Wales, in a high-performance Fireball sailing dinghy. Eduardo was holding onto the tiller with a determined grimace while John hiked out on the trapeze, a thin wire rope, so his weight would keep the boat from blowing over in the strong winds. The only part of John's body touching the boat were the balls of his feet. Despite the loud noise of the wind whipping through the rigging, making conversation impossible, John could discern the joyful whooping and laughter of his best friend, Eduardo, as they exhilaratingly rode down the massive waves.

Their fearlessness towards mortality was evident given their youth, with their primary aim of creating as much excitement as possible. During their breaks in the morning classes, all they could discuss was the excitement of the adrenaline-fuelled afternoon that lay ahead. The conditions were ideal for sailing, so they knew it would be a fantastic day on the water.

Suddenly, the bow of the Fireball plowed into an enormous wall of water, likely two waves piled onto each other, doubling the waves' typical height. In an instant, the dinghy stopped its forward movement. John could feel his body fly forward through the air, but he remained attached to the rigging, with the trapeze harness firmly secured to his midriff. Like a yo-yo on a string, his body sprung back into the mainsail, toppling the sailboat.

John hit the water violently. A load of seawater rushed up his nostrils from the violent impact. When his life jacket catapulted to the surface and popped his head above the water, he could see Eduardo climbing onto the keel to bring the boat upright. In less than 30 seconds, with Eduardo once again holding the tiller, John was climbing back onto the now up-righted sailboat. They were off, screaming down the waves, John back on the trapeze with Eduardo's delightful hooting and hollering in the wind.

"I guess you didn't expect to have such a crazy roommate when they put us together two years ago," said Eduardo as they pulled the Fireball up the slipway now secured on a trailer.

"That was the most excitement I've ever had on the ocean and it's a bonus I'm still alive to talk about it," said John. "Where did you learn to sail like that?"

"My father loves ocean racing. He has an 80-foot sailboat with 25 crew to race it. He's too bossy for my liking, so the captain of the boat would take me on the water in these Fireball two-person dinghies. That's how I learned from age six. I find the smaller sailboats a lot more exhilarating. I can be my own boss, and I don't have to listen to my dad."

They sat on the stone wall in their wetsuits and glanced at

the sea. The wind had picked up, and the waves were bigger. "You know, I felt safe out there with you even after we had capsized," said John. "You knew exactly what to do and how far to push the boat. That's not something I could say with some others on the sailing team."

Eduardo went silent. "I wish the rest of my life would go as well. You are so lucky, heading back to Canada to become a doctor. You know what you want, and your parents are your biggest fans. My father has big plans for me to take over his company. He's sending me to Princeton to learn how. What he doesn't know is that I switched out of business school and I'm in the philosophy program. I need to find myself, John. How is it so easy for you?"

John thought about that for a moment before answering. "I'm just following the path that my heart is guiding me, like a compass pointing me in my true direction. I've always wanted to be a doctor. For me, it is just one foot in front of the other until I attain my goal."

"I wish I could say the same. My compass doesn't point in the same direction as yours. I need to find my place in life. I'm not going to allow my father to tell me what that place should be."

"We've talked about this before. You need to completely accept that you are gay and not be afraid of living your life as a gay man. You were born like that. It wasn't something you chose or asked for. This is the new millennium now, and you need to get with the program."

"I wish my family were as accepting as you. There is no way they will see things that way. I'd rather keep this from them."

John sat quietly as they looked out on the tempest the wind had created. The tide had risen, and the waves were bouncing off the seawall, sending plumes of water 20 feet in the air and filling their nostrils with sharp brininess. Noise from the waves crashing into the solid wall made for difficult conversation. "They might surprise you," said John between a set. "My parents have always told me that their love for me will always overcome any obstacle that is thrown my way. I suspect your parents love you just as much. You need to give them the chance. I am certain if I were gay, and I told my family, they would embrace me with open arms and ask me what they could do to help."

Eduardo looked at John with sadness in his eyes. "You live in a fantasy world. I come from a privileged one and they expect me to conform in all aspects of life. They will tell me to be a good Catholic boy and marry a pretty Italian girl. If I tell them to shove that existence up their asses, they'll boot me out of their lives."

"You'll find your way, Eduardo. You are a good person and have been a great friend to me." John went quiet as an enormous wave crashed into the wall with a resounding thud, shaking where they sat. "While you are sorting out your life's direction, tell me something. Why is it that all the girls here love hanging out with you? Do I have to pretend to be gay to get that kind of attention?"

"Ha ha," laughed Eduardo. "Is that all you straight guys think about? They feel safe with me. They know we can be friends without me saying anything. It's almost as if guys like you barrel into their space with neon lights flashing that say, 'I just want to get laid.' They pick up on your non-verbal clues within seconds."

"You have a lot to teach me about women! Kind of ironic, isn't it? You can have any woman you want without even putting any effort into it. With me, it's a life struggle just to get them to talk to me. Life is so unfair!"

Eduardo looked out at the ocean, now a chaotic mess of white water and spray that was flying off the top of the mountainous waves horizontally. The weather had deteriorated to the point where it wouldn't be safe on the water in a small sailboat. "Yes," he said, looking into the distance, "life is unfair."

Chapter Four

Kathmandu's Tribhuvan International Airport was chaotic. Suzie and John were waiting in a long line to get a visa. Several weeks before they'd left Toronto, they'd gone to the Nepal government website, which suggested getting a visa before arrival, but there were numerous issues with the online process even after they had completed the required fields. As they looked at the forms, they noticed the warnings telling them they hadn't completed them correctly. After spending half an hour trying to correct the problem, they called the Canadian consulate in Ottawa, which suggested they could get the visa at the customs and immigration booth at the airport, but they would need to have $120 each in cash.

As John looked around, he noticed that the travellers with pre-arranged visas had a significant advantage—they were swiftly waved through the shorter line. He spotted Eduardo scooting past the immigration officers in the visa line and their eyes met. Eduardo smiled and then waved before disappearing down the hallway to the baggage collection carousel.

John sighed. He wondered whether Eduardo's motivation to climb Everest stemmed from a desire to conquer a daunting challenge and find personal validation, or if it was driven by a death wish for an end to his hardships. It had always fascinated John that one could never know what drove people's behaviours. During his tenure as chief of surgery, he thought a great deal about this. While it may be easy for others to judge a surgeon with disruptive behaviour as a jerk for raising their voice at a scrub nurse for a minor mistake, John would take a more nuanced approach by seeking to uncover the underlying motivations behind such actions.

High levels of stress characterized the surgical environment, and it was common for surgeons to perceive complications as a direct attack on their personal character. If problems arose during surgery, the stakes were high, potentially resulting in fatal consequences. Naturally, it wasn't uncommon for blame to be directed towards the surgeon, both from patients and even their colleagues. As part of surgical training, it was crucial to maintain composure and clarity of thought, even in the face of difficult situations.

Surgeons frequently became unravelled because of other stressful events in their life, too. Substance abuse was high on the list, but so were family issues, such as divorce or child-related problems. Although surgeons enjoyed a good income, many had financial problems. Shortly after a disruptive incident had taken place, John would arrange a meeting with the surgeon. Through his developed techniques, he could encourage the doctor to open up about the events that led to the uncharacteristic behaviour. Then John would offer his help in getting them back on track. If only he could spend more time with Eduardo, he might have been able to help him, too.

The queue moved faster than expected, so after paying for the tourist visa and getting their passports stamped, John and Suzie retrieved their luggage. Upon entering the arrivals lounge, they immediately noticed a short man in white pants and a white shirt holding a sign with their names. He smiled as they approached him.

"Dr. Hegland?" the man asked them. John nodded in affirmation. "I'm here to drive you to the hotel. Welcome to Kathmandu."

The man grabbed their bags and rolled them into the waiting black SUV. It was a short drive to the Hyatt Regency Kathmandu, which was surrounded by stupas and gilded monasteries—all back dropped by towering mountains. The surgical meetings would start tomorrow at the conference centre next door. Suzie and John checked into their luxury room. The lengthy journey left both feeling exhausted. Following their shower, they climbed into bed for a quick nap before joining the rest for dinner.

Mathew, John's surgical fellow, had arrived a day earlier. He was already sitting at the table engaged in conversation with Jerico, organizer of the surgical conference. John watched as Mathew's face broke into a warm smile at something Jerico had said. Mathew, in his early thirties, had close-cropped black hair consistent two-day-old growth of facial hair, which appeared unchanged day after day. His thick and muscular body seemed to belie his soft-spoken mannerisms, which had undoubtedly captivated Jerico. Mathew commanded the calm presence of someone who was always in control of his emotions.

John first encountered Mathew when the younger man was a medical student doing his surgery rotation and was assigned to him. Mathew had initially expressed interest in family medicine, but he quickly discovered that the adrenaline and excitement of surgery captivated him more. Just as he effortlessly conquered video games, laparoscopic surgery skills came naturally to him. During Mathew's demanding five-year surgical residency, it amazed John at his progression from novice to proficient surgeon. The hospital hired Mathew as the minimally invasive surgery fellow after he successfully completed the surgery exams.

John had invited Mathew to partake in the conference to give some talks about robotic surgery. Mathew had better surgical skills using a robot than most of the staff surgeons, so he was a good fit to present at the international meeting. The experience would enhance Mathew's resume and make him more competitive in job applications.

Mathew's face lit up as he saw John and Suzie. He quickly stood up and embraced them both. "Great to see you!" he exclaimed. "I'm glad I got here early. I wanted to be rested for my talk!"

"It's good to see you too, Mathew," said John as they joined him and Jerico. He looked over at the stocky man, who was just over five feet. "Hi, Jerico." The pair shook hands and Jerico smiled and nodded at Suzie. He wore thick glasses and had a round, pleasant face.

Jerico was originally from Mainland China, but had immigrated to Canada 25 years ago, searching for a better life. He spoke English with a thick Mandarin accent. When he talked quickly, as was his custom, John found it difficult to understand what he was saying. Today was no exception.

"Good to see you, John," he said. "We have a very good program. A lot of participants. Very good."

Jerico had organized the meeting with an international panel of experts to discuss a wide range of topics, including rectal cancer, bariatric surgery, and gynecology surgery. John knew it was all business for Jerico. With its wide advertising, the international meeting drew participants from every corner of the globe. Jerico charged a fee of $800 to attend, but the bulk of his profits came from organizing extra-curricular activities, including a range of exciting tours and events. That was what attracted the doctors to come from so far away, plus they could write off the trip as a business expense.

Among the many things that enticed John to partake in the Kathmandu conference, it was the helicopter ride to the base camp of Mount Everest that held a special allure. He'd dreamed about climbing Mount Everest since he was 10. John would climb up the small jungle gym in the local park and pretend he was scaling the mighty mountain. One day, he scrambled up onto the roof of the garage. He used the drainpipe as a handle to pull himself up. When he got to the top, he stood up on the edge of the eaves trough and looked down.

John felt the ground spin around him. He suddenly felt nauseated. He felt himself fall through the air as if in a dream.

The bushes at the edge of the garage acted as a protective barrier, sparing him from a major injury but leaving him with a few scratches. As he looked up at the sky, trying to understand what had happened, it was then that he realized he was afraid of heights.

John had battled with this phobia all his life. Despite his ability to fly in both planes and helicopters without experiencing dizziness, as soon as there was nothing but air separating him from the ground at a height exceeding 10 feet, he would suddenly feel the earth spinning and quickly become overwhelmed with nausea.

To overcome his fear, he explored desensitization techniques, which included bungee jumping off a bridge, but the intensity of the experience caused him to nearly lose consciousness as fear surged through him when he plummeted to the ground. Cognitive behavioural therapy (CBT) was a technique of increased mindfulness he tried to help guide him through the irrational fear of heights. Even after three months of CBT, if he were to ascend to the top rung of a ladder, the dizziness would come back.

It occurred to John that maybe his fear of heights was the reason he found Mount Everest so captivating. Imagining standing on the tallest mountain in the world without feeling any dizziness while looking down at the world below, John would realize that he possessed the strength and resilience to overcome any obstacle that life could hurl in his path. He now knew that he'd never overcome his fear of heights. By working through his weaknesses and constantly striving to improve himself was how he gained confidence and strength from each new opportunity that came his way.

Jerico said, "Thanks for coming, John. It is going to be a great conference, just like the four other trips in China we organized over the past few years."

"Sounds great, Jerico," said John. "But we've travelled to China *five* times with you. Without exception, every trip was nothing short of phenomenal. Remember the action-packed itinerary last time? Seeing the iconic Great Wall of China, the historical wonder of Xian's Terracotta Warriors, the majestic Yellow Mountain, and many more captivating sights. How could I miss the opportunity for an all-expenses-paid trip to China, where not only do I get to witness the wonders of China, but the experiences also have boosted my reputation as a renowned speaker on the global stage?"

"This year you brought Mathew with you. You need to put him to work!"

"I intend to. Instead of me doing the surgery, this time I am going to let him perform the laparoscopic and robotic techniques he's learned from my team of surgeons. The Chinese surgeons loved it when I agreed to participate in surgery to help them learn advanced laparoscopic techniques and manoeuvres that would enhance their surgical skills. Mathew is one of the strongest MIS fellows we have had in years. I have him doing a case for tomorrow's conference for the Nepalese Surgical Society."

"Very good. I'm very pleased. However, I couldn't help but notice it took little for me to convince you to agree to journey to Kathmandu. If I had known about Mathew, I would have bypassed you completely. He seems very balanced."

"Ha ha," laughed John. "You find me unbalanced? Wait until we are at base camp and we will see whether it is you or me that is the most mentally stable!"

The server arrived with their dinner. Because of the frequent power outages in Nepal, the consensus was to avoid eating meat since the refrigeration was not reliable. Tonight's meal consisted of the Nepali dish *dal bhat*, made from lentils, paired with steamed rice, vegetables and achar, a spicy sauce. For dessert, they had *yomari*, a delightful dumpling made from rice flour filled with sweet taffy. Everything was exceptional.

They bid each other goodnight and headed to their rooms.

Chapter Five

John observed with a deep sense of pride as he watched Mathew complete the gastric bypass surgery. In less than an hour, Mathew had flawlessly performed the procedure while John provided help. The patient had a classification of severe obesity with a BMI of 40. Alongside sleep apnea, diabetes, and hypertension, the patient's medical conditions also included a severe fatty liver with early cirrhosis. In Mathew's steady hands, the laparoscopic instruments glided across the screen with precision and grace, as if they were performing a meticulously choreographed dance routine to a complicated musical composition. John was confident that the surgery could not have been conducted any more skillfully if he had performed it himself.

"That was amazing," exclaimed Dr. Pansour. "I could never do one in less than three hours. I knew it would be helpful for our bariatric team in Nepal to watch. Could we review the video afterwards? I have a few questions."

John looked up from the operating table and nodded. "It is always a good idea to evaluate the cases. Mathew has already pointed out to me a few minor technical issues he had, so there is plenty to discuss." John left the operating table, peeled off his gloves and gown, and joined Dr. Pansour standing in the corner.

"You know," said Dr. Pansour, "Obesity has only become a

problem in Nepal since the country has become westernized. Starbucks, McDonald's, and Kentucky Fried Chicken are to blame. And with the internet, more people are sitting on their butts all day and snacking on junk food."

"We have the same issues in Toronto," said John. "Instead of playing soccer, the kids are sedentary and engrossed in video games. Whether you're in one country or another, things are the same everywhere."

Dr. Pansour laughed. "Thanks for the surgical lesson. Would you have time to review the videos when you get back from your helicopter ride tomorrow?"

"Absolutely. We better head to the lecture hall. My talk begins in 30 minutes, and I must load my presentation."

The two of them walked to the conference centre and joined the crowd of surgeons on the midmorning coffee break. As Dr. Pansour conversed with a familiar individual, John made his way into the lecture hall, intending to transfer his presentation onto the computer in the conference room. He stood patiently at the podium, watching as the physicians made their way back after the coffee break had ended. After everyone had found their places and the room fell into a calm hush, John started his presentation in front of 200 physicians.

He spoke about how morbid obesity surgery currently ranks

among the most frequently conducted surgeries across the globe. John's talk discussed how weight-loss surgery would improve fertility in women by curing polycystic ovarian syndrome. In men, weight-loss surgery improved spermatic motility and improved testosterone production. The current evidence strongly supports the notion that weight-loss surgery, when undergone by both men and women, can significantly decrease the likelihood of obesity in their children. In his concluding remarks, John emphasized that weight-loss surgery had the potential to eliminate obesity for future generations, highlighting its significance on par with other global challenges like climate change and poverty.

After it was over, the audience applauded politely. John felt a sense of accomplishment that his talk was well-received and successful.

Now Mathew was up. His talk on robotic surgery and rectal cancer generated even greater interest among the audience when he proposed the idea of integrating artificial intelligence into the robot's operations. "AI, having analyzed data from thousands of rectal operations, can alert the surgeon if the dissection is approaching critical structures like the ureter or pelvic nerves," explained Mathew. "The introduction of this technology brings a whole new dimension of safety to the field of surgery."

Mathew expertly fielded many questions that were asked.

His competence delighted John in answering every single question. "Great talk," said John as he made his way from the podium.

"Thanks!" said Mathew. "This is my first international meeting where I'm giving a presentation. I'm pleased with how it went."

John was about to say something to Mathew when he felt someone tap him on the shoulder. "Dr. Hegland," said the man. "My name is Peter Polanski."

John swiftly turned around to face the man, who wore a pleasant smile on his face. His beard, along with his long hair that was tied in a ponytail, both had a vibrant red colour. He was shorter than John's six-two height by a few inches. With his ruddy complexion, it was evident that he was no stranger to the great outdoors.

"I am an emergency doctor at UHN in Toronto," Peter said, extending his hand. "It is a pleasure to meet you."

With a firm and confident grip, the handshake conveyed a sense of strength and assurance. His body looked solid and square. His bicep muscles bulged against the taut T-shirt's fabric.

John reciprocated the smile. "I also find it a great pleasure to meet you."

"I gave a talk at the same time as you in a different room," said Peter. "I am sorry I missed yours."

"What was your talk about?" asked John.

"I discussed the treatment of high-altitude sickness, pulmonary edema, and cerebral edema. A few years ago, I established the emergency hospital at Everest Base Camp, and I return here for two months every spring climbing season. My partner comes in October to run the hospital for the fall climbing season."

"Hey," said John, excitedly. "We're flying to base camp tomorrow by helicopter. Could you show us around the hospital?"

"Sure thing," said Peter. "I am leaving first thing in the morning, so I should be up there when you arrive."

"Can you tell me something?" asked John. "We have just come from Toronto. Base camp is at 5,280 meters. I know that acclimatization usually takes six weeks. Is there a chance we'll face trouble because we haven't taken the time to adjust?"

"Ha," laughed Peter. "You'll be there for less than half an hour. In just about three minutes, you can tour the hospital, snap some pictures, and then be on your way in the helicopter. While you may experience breathlessness, it is unlikely to develop high-altitude sickness in such a brief period."

"As I recall, headaches are common," said John. "Cerebral

edema could cause incoordination or confusion and in extreme cases, unconsciousness and death."

"For such a brief visit, take some Diamox and Advil," suggested Peter. "That should take care of the headaches. You are unlikely to run into altitude sickness. Even if you get a mild headache, it will be worth it. You will never experience the Himalayas like this in your lifetime. The views are magnificent."

"What types of medical emergencies does the hospital commonly treat?" asked Mathew, fascinated by the conversation.

"Oh, anything from broken bones to dysentery from eating contaminated food," answered Peter. "Every year there is a death from altitude sickness, usually pulmonary edema. If the helicopter cannot get to base camp because of bad weather, there is not much we can do to help them. To provide immediate medical assistance, we administer dexamethasone and Lasix while intubating the patient, ensuring high oxygen delivery with a portable ventilator until further help arrives. While cerebral edema tends to dissipate rapidly upon descending to lower altitudes, pulmonary edema proves to be much more stubborn."

John's cell phone buzzed. It was Suzie texting him, wondering what he was up to. "Meet me in the conference room lobby," he replied to her. "There is someone I want you to meet."

"Peter," said John, "I want to introduce you to Suzie, my

significant other. She will meet us in the lobby."

The trio walked to the lobby and after waiting less than three minutes, Suzie arrived. John introduced her to Peter. "Very nice to meet you," he said, looking directly into Suzie's eyes. John watched as Suzie shook his hand, saying nothing. A subtle shudder ran through her body that only he would detect. Her eyes seemed to penetrate through to the back of Peter's head. John observed as Peter shifted his gaze away while shaking his head uncomfortably.

After bidding farewell and making plans to reunite at Everest Base Camp the next day, Peter left. John turned to Suzie and said, "He's going to show us around the hospital at base camp in the morning. We'll only have time for pictures, and then we'll get back in the helicopter before we succumb to altitude sickness."

Initially, Suzie remained quiet. "Hey honey, what's up?" asked John. "Is it the jet lag?"

"John," said Suzie with a worried look, "he is not to be trusted. He is going to cause us problems."

John was aghast. "How can you be so sure? You met him for less than 30 seconds! What is it about him that makes you think that?"

"I don't know where it comes from, but my intuition has never failed us before," said Suzie. "He's trouble. I think you should stay away from him."

Chapter Six

Leaving John, Suzie, and Mathew in the conference room lobby, Peter's mind drifted to the hospital he had established at base camp. Two years ago, it was teetering on the edge of financial ruin, but now Peter was hopeful it would survive. It was crucial to have the hospital to support the dangerous but lucrative expeditions. Five major companies offered mountaineer guides up Mount Everest with westerners willing to spend anywhere from $75,000 to $150,000 for the eight-week visit to Nepal. The outfitters' success depended on clients making it to the summit.

The trek from Lukla, the closest airport to Everest Base Camp, would span 15 days, providing ample time for them to adjust to the altitude. Then the climbers would set off on a demanding trek to Camp 1, immersing themselves in the rugged terrain of the Khumbu Icefalls before returning to base. Throughout the following month, they steadily climbed, reaching higher altitudes until they finally reached Camp 4. Only then would they be ready to make the final ascent to the summit.

Despite Peter's efforts to pitch the hospital concept to the mountaineer guide companies, they hesitated to provide financial support because of their own precarious financial situations. They suggested he charge the clients directly for any medical services. Unfortunately, the local climbing community of Sherpas couldn't afford to visit the hospital, even though they were the ones who needed it the most. At base camp during the height of the climbing season, as many as 1,000 campers stayed for up to two months. Peter suggested they pay a $100 medical insurance fee, but most felt the $11,000 climbing permit per visitor should cover it.

Financial relief came from the most unlikely source. Canadian entrepreneur Jerico Chang generously pledged $1 million to cover the hospital's operational costs for the next decade. In return, he wanted control of the hospital operations and 60 per cent share of the profits. Peter felt there was little risk: there were no profits. Initially, everything went smoothly as Jerico equipped the hospital with state-of-the-art high-altitude resuscitation gear. The deal included a provision where Sherpas involved in Everest expeditions received free medical care, while the doctors received a small stipend. Laughing at the idiotic arrangement, Peter couldn't help but shake his head, knowing that profits were unlikely in the foreseeable future, yet confident that his hospital would thrive.

During Peter's two-month stay at base camp in Nepal this year, he witnessed his hospital's remarkable achievement as it gained international recognition for its ground-breaking work in treating high altitude sickness. Institutions constantly sought him out, eager to have him share his knowledge by lecturing on the topic throughout the year. For Peter, this was his dream come true. International recognition and living in the most exciting environment on the planet.

Jerico would visit the hospital once every two weeks by helicopter. He would bring in fresh supplies and take out the old equipment and the garbage. There was a small storage room next to the hospital where the used oxygen bottles and other old equipment lay until the helicopter came.

Late one night, Peter was intrigued by an unusual sound that pierced the quiet of the small hospital tent, so he ventured out to investigate. Surprised by the noise emanating from the storage room, Peter cautiously approached, straining to decipher the mysterious sounds that filled the air. When he opened the door he saw a Sherpa, burdened by a heavy pack secured to his forehead, make his way to a corner where he laid the pack down. Peter recognized him.

"Pesang?" asked Peter. "What are you doing here? I would have thought you'd be getting the ropes ready on the mountain for the climbers."

Startled by the unexpected intrusion, Pesang swiftly turned his body to meet Peter's gaze. "Jerico asked me to leave this stuff for him. He is coming tomorrow to clean out all this garbage."

"What's in the bag?" asked Peter.

Without uttering a single word, Pesang turned away and

exited through the door, stepping out into the chilly embrace of the mountain night air.

Peter stared at the closed door for a moment before he walked towards the bag. The weight was too much for him to lift, and he marvelled at how the Sherpas managed to carry such loads on their heads for days on end. The canvas bag had a combination lock on one end, adding an extra layer of security to keep the ties tightly bound. Peter's headlamp illuminated the contents of a plastic bag as he peeked through the small opening between the ties.

There appeared to be a black tarry substance inside. With a small knife in hand, he carefully made a small cut into the plastic and cautiously inserted his index finger. The sticky black stuff coated his finger. It had a smell resembling vinegar, strong and acidic. When he tasted it, he discovered it had a surprisingly sweet flavour.

In an instant, he realized what he was looking at, sending a chill down his spine. Black heroin. Peter's pulse raced. He felt a sense of urgency and a desperate need for more air. There were reports in the news that Nepal had a booming opium poppy industry. Peter was aware of this, but never expected to have a load of black heroin in his hospital. It was at that precise moment when he realized the purpose behind Jerico's $1 million investment in his hospital. Peter felt dizzy. His legs wobbled, and he sat down on the floor next to the bag. His head was spinning, and he felt a wave of nausea wash over him.

Peter vividly remembered the terrible argument he'd had with Jerico the day after finding the bag, when Jerico arrived in a helicopter to collect his stash. He briefly considered keeping silent about the heroin, weighing the consequences in his mind. Even though Jerico owned the clinic, Peter still regarded it as his own. He had poured his heart and soul into constructing it, giving it every ounce of his energy. Incorporating it as a conduit for heroin was not part of his plan. But now that he knew, he couldn't remain silent and do nothing.

Jerico had just arrived at base camp and was walking towards the storage shed.

Peter confronted him. "I refuse to allow you to use my ER clinic as a drug running operation," he said, raising his voice. His eyes flashed with defiance.

Jerico stopped in his tracks, turned, and glared at Peter. "You little shit. It's not up to you to dictate what I can or cannot do. Do you really think you can stop me?" Jerico turned around and walked to the storage shed.

Peter was fuming and followed him. "This medical clinic is a world class internationally recognized facility," he said, his red hair catching the wind adding to his angry demeanour. "This is the only standalone operation worldwide dedicated to advancing our understanding of high-altitude sickness, and I won't let you undermine the progress I've made."

Jerico went silent as he glared at the raging man in front of him. Then a smile spread across his face. Peter was confused. Jerico continued. "You can choose what you wish to do. Either let me continue to conduct my business, or you can go to jail."

"What… What are you talking about?"

"Last year you fraudulently billed the Nepalese Ministry of Health $98,000 for dialysis. The patient's name was…" Jerico took out his phone and scrolled. "Here it is. Lhakpa Sherpa. On May 3 of last year, you billed dialysis services that you never provided. He died on April 30."

Peter frowned, remembering the circumstances. He had looked after him in the clinic. The son of Lhakpa worked for the minister of health; it was he who had suggested the financial transaction. The clinic received a new ventilator with the money. The son had told him this kind of thing happened all the time and no one would ever find out. They did not have the resources at the ministry to do a proper audit, he had explained.

"I did nothing wrong!" shouted Peter.

"You can collect your stuff and get the fuck out of here

then," shouted Jerico. "You agreed to let me run the show here, so if you don't like it, leave!"

Peter fixed his gaze on Jerico's pilot, his eyes following every movement as the canvas bag he carried got loaded onto the helicopter. The chopper took off. As he glared at the helicopter window, watching Jerico fly away, he refrained from uttering any words. He could see his dreams slipping away. Jerico, being cunning and resourceful, had used his hospital to smuggle heroin, cleverly concealing it within the medical waste, fully aware that his actions would go unquestioned. Since Peter had dedicated much of his emotional energy to the ER hospital, and now that there were many people relying on its services, he felt compelled to stay.

The sound of Peter's cell phone buzzing snapped him back to the present moment. It was a message from Jerico, inviting him to a meeting in his hotel room. Peter sighed. *What now? Haven't I done enough for that ungrateful slime?*

Peter took the elevator to Jerico's room and knocked on the door. Naturally Jerico's "room" was a luxurious suite with a spacious living room, outfitted with a comfortable sofa and a cozy fireplace, where a wood fire was ablaze. Another man, in his late fifties with short grey hair, sat on the sofa, mesmerized by the crackling fire, as he leisurely sipped on a glass filled with ice and a golden-hued liquid. Jerico led Peter to another chair next to the sofa, motioning for him to sit, but the man didn't even bother to look up.

"Peter," said Jerico. "Thanks for coming."

Peter gazed at him and said nothing. Not only did Jerico neglect to offer him a drink, but he also failed to introduce him to the grey-haired man.

"Why did you want to see me?" Peter asked after a moment of silence.

Jerico glanced at the man on the sofa, then focused his attention back on Peter.

"There will be an accident of sorts on the mountain tomorrow," explained Jerico. "The man will suffer significant injuries. You must not offer him any medical assistance. He is to die on the mountain."

"Jerico," Peter replied in a calm voice, trying his best to maintain composure, "it is not reasonable to expect a doctor to look away from someone who gets injured. We must assist anyone, without regard to their gender, race, or religion. I cannot comply with your request and must decline."

"I was worried you might say that." Jerico pulled out his cell phone and scrolled. When he found what he was looking for, he showed Peter. It was a picture of Peter's parents walking up the wooden steps of their house in Toronto. His father was wearing a deerstalker cap, the kind fashioned by his hero, Sherlock Holmes, as he held his mother's hand so she wouldn't slip on the ice that glistened in the sun. His mother was gazing at her husband with a shine in her eyes. The photo had captured a moment of tenderness between them. Peter's heart skipped a beat.

"We wouldn't want anything to happen to them, would we?"

Chapter Seven

At the early hour of 4 a.m., the alarm went off, disrupting the peaceful silence. Startled, John shot up in bed, his senses immediately alert. He turned off the blaring alarm and blinked at the bright red numbers on the clock, finally realizing where he was. They had planned to rendezvous at the hotel lobby at 4:30 to catch a taxi to the heliport. John woke up Suzie. After getting out of bed, Suzie bundled up in warm layers, preparing herself for the anticipated cold at base camp. John did the same. They both came prepared for the winter weather, with their sturdy winter boots, insulated snow pants, and cozy Gore-tex coats.

Suzie put her arms around John and said, "Honey, are you sure you want to do this? I can already detect your anxiety, and we haven't even left the room."

John glanced at Suzie's concerned face. "I'm good," he said as he tried to brush away her concerns. "After years of therapy, I have conquered my fear of heights. I am ready to test it in real time."

Suzie broke into a raucous laugh. "Tell me another one, you moron. You are sweating anxiety pheromones in buckets right now. We don't have to go. Let's tell Jerico we are unwell and crawl back into bed."

John smiled. "I can do this, Suzie. It is what I have always dreamed about. Base camp at Mount Everest during climbing season. Besides, Peter is expecting to show us around Everest ER. I can't let that opportunity pass. I'm good. Honest."

Suzie just shook her head and disentangled herself from John. "OK. Macho man. Don't expect me to bail you out when you have a panic attack at 2,000 feet above the ground."

Jerico and Mathew were in the hotel lobby when John and Suzie arrived. The concierge waved to them, indicating the arrival of the taxi. The ride to the heliport took less than 20 minutes. When they arrived at the terminal, they found the helicopter parked on the tarmac.

As the sun rose, its rays filtered in and cast a beautiful light. The sky stretched out above, a vibrant shade of blue with not a single cloud in sight. As the helicopter engine roared to life, the four passengers made their way towards the aircraft's door, instinctively ducking their heads to avoid the helicopter's wings. Once they fastened their seatbelts, they felt a slight jolt as the aircraft took off. As they looked down, John could make out the vibrant city of Kathmandu stirring with activity in the early morning traffic.

Within minutes, they were soaring over a breathtaking valley surrounded by towering cliffs. Along the cliffs stood majestic trees with lush green foliage framing the path to the river, which cascaded with rapid currents, creating a mesmerizing sight as its white rapids flowed through the valley. John fixed his eyes on the window and witnessed the landscape below gradually lose its vibrancy and succumb to a barrenness as they soared above the tree line. After 30 minutes, the pilot made an announcement they could hear through their headphones. "We'll be landing at Lukla Airport shortly. Please remain seated while we refuel. We will depart in 10 minutes after touchdown."

Once landed, Jerico said, "This is one of the most dangerous airports in the world. The runways are short and at one end there is a cliff. Just last year, a twin-engine plane crashed into a helicopter, killing three people."

Suzie looked at Jerico with a concerned look. "Why are you telling us this?" she asked. "John is already terrified of heights. There is no need to add to his anxiety."

Jerico laughed. "It's all part of the adventure," he explained. "You have nothing to worry about. Every two weeks during the climbing season, I make my way up to base camp by helicopter to collect the medical waste from the hospital, surrounded by breathtaking mountain views. I have turned it into a business. Nothing has ever happened to me. The pilots are very careful."

John said. "I'm fine. My fear of heights only surfaces when I find myself standing on a sheer cliff, with nothing but open space below. As I sit in the helicopter, I can't help but marvel at the breathtaking views that surround me. I am feeling completely at ease."

Suzie leaned over, her voice barely audible, and whispered in his ear, "That is complete bullshit. The smell of your anxiety is overpowering, reaching my nostrils, and making me uneasy. You can hardly wait until this is over."

John turned to her and smiled. "You are right," he chuckled, his nervous laughter filling the cockpit. "I consider this to be part of my desensitization therapy. Soon I'll want to take you paragliding."

Suzie laughed and jokingly replied, "There is no chance of that happening in this lifetime."

Having spent 10 minutes on the ground, they ascended back into the air, embarking on a 30-minute flight that would ultimately lead them to the base camp. As the helicopter ascended towards the Khumbu Icefall, the breathtaking sight of Mount Everest unfolded before their eyes. The jet stream at the top caused the magnificent mountain to flare with a wisp of snow and ice on its summit. As the helicopter approached base camp, they could see the brightly coloured tents that extended for about half a kilometre along the Khumbu Icefall.

Jerico pointed to something on the ground, but John could not hear what he said above the aircraft noise. The helicopter, which had been circling above, eventually descended and landed gracefully on a patch of flat rocks that had a red and white windsock placed nearby to show the wind's direction.

"You've got 15 minutes at base camp before we take off," said the pilot. "If any of you are interested in the hospital, you can easily spot it as the first tent on the left."

Upon landing the helicopter, they all swiftly disembarked and walked together towards the white tent with Everest ER written on the side. John immediately noticed how short of breath he was after only a few steps. They were at 17,598 feet. Jerico led the way and opened the door of the tent. Peter was sitting at the desk in the reception area. He stood up with a smile and said, "Welcome to Everest ER."

"Wow," exclaimed John, "I wasn't expecting a tent hospital!"

"We set this up twice a year during the climbing season," said Peter. "Our clinic operates for two months in both the spring and fall, during which we are able to treat around 650 patients."

With a look of amazement, John glanced around the tent, taking in every detail. In one corner were many oxygen cylinders piled up. Further down, a ventilator was pushed up against the wall. Behind a locked glass cabinet, drugs were stored in small boxes that were meticulously labelled.

"I'll give you the 30-second tour," said Peter. He started walking towards the back of the tent. Some improvised white drapes concealed a hospital bed, with an IV pole holding a bag of normal saline solution in case they needed it in a hurry. "This is the only room we have to treat emergencies."

John, Suzie, and Mathew followed Peter as he exited out a back entrance.

"Here is our storage room," said Peter, as the helicopter pilot walked out, carrying black plastic bags filled with used medical supplies. They peeked inside the room as the pilot threw the bags into the back of the helicopter. The next item he grabbed was a canvas duffle. It was clearly heavy, the weight evident as he placed the strap on his head and made his way back to the helicopter. Struggling to lift it, he looked to Jerico, who was waiting by the helicopter door, for help in throwing it in.

"We leave in 10 minutes," shouted the pilot.

"Peter," said John, passing his phone to the red-headed doctor. "Take a picture of me, Mathew, and Suzie in front of the tent with Everest in the background." He took several pictures of them, then continued the tour.

"This is where I sleep; over here," said Peter as he pointed to a yellow tent next to the hospital tent. "I need to be ready at a moment's notice." Inside was a compact cot with a thick sleeping bag on top. A small heater, carefully positioned in a corner, diligently fought against the freezing mountain air, creating a warm and inviting atmosphere within the tent. They took some more pictures.

Just as they entered the hospital tent, Peter's Iridium satellite phone went off. He walked over to a small desk and pinched a button. From the desk speaker a voice said, "Hello, Peter?"

"Yes, it's me," answered Peter.

"I'm calling from Camp 1. There is a medical emergency that I would like to discuss with you. We have a climber, Eduardo Rattazzi, who we just witnessed having a seizure. He had fallen and his arm was hanging at an unusual angle. I think he broke it."

John's heart skipped a beat as soon as he heard his friend's name. As anxiety built in his chest, he felt a tightness constricting his breath. It hadn't even been two full days since they had last met, but it already felt like a distant memory. He could not accept that Eduardo had already become entangled in trouble. John leaned in closer to the speakerphone, eager to catch every word.

"He probably has high-altitude cerebral edema," said Peter.

"I don't think so," said the voice. "Until the seizure occurred, he was completely clearheaded and coherent. There was neither incoordination nor any sign of confusion. As he lost his balance and fell, his body immediately twitched uncontrollably, and his eyes rolled back into his head. Although his breathing had resumed, he remained completely unresponsive to any attempts to wake him up."

"You need to bring him back to base camp," said Peter.

There was silence on the other end of the line. "We do not have a medivac sled. The search and rescue team are up on the mountain dealing with another emergency. With a storm approaching, we are uncertain whether there is enough time to descend to base camp, retrieve a medivac sled, and bring him down before the storm hits. Besides, the ice doctors have cautioned us that the bridges across the crevices on Khumbu ice fields are unstable and can only hold one climber at a time. Can't you come up to us?"

Peter looked at Suzie and John. "I cannot come up and you know that. Medical personnel are required to always remain at base camp. You'll have to manage until we can send someone. Can you call me back in 20 minutes?" asked Peter.

John felt numb. His school mate from many years ago was in trouble. "Can't we pick him up in the helicopter?" he asked.

"Let's go talk to the pilot," suggested Suzie. In a flurry of movement, the couple darted out of the hospital tent. As John rushed out, he could sense Peter's penetrating stare from the small desk, sending a shiver down his spine.

"There they are!" exclaimed John, as he urgently pointed towards Jerico and the helicopter pilot, who were both standing next to the passenger door. Suzie and John rushed over to them.

John relayed the information that he heard on Peter's satellite phone to the pilot while Jerico listened. Looking directly at Jerico, the pilot's eyes held a silent plea for guidance, as if he was unsure of how to proceed. Jerico's head shook ever so slightly, almost undetectable. John was sure Suzie had noticed, too.

"We need to help my friend Eduardo," pleaded John. "Can you fly to Camp 1?"

"Not possible," said the pilot. "We need to get off the mountain now; they only allow us to stay for a maximum of 30 minutes. To stay longer, you need to apply for a permit. I am sorry; we cannot help him."

"You need to leave this to the professionals," said Jerico. "They are used to managing all kinds of medical emergencies on the mountain. We need to leave now, so please board the helicopter."

Mathew and Suzie climbed into the helicopter. John watched, unable to move. Then he turned to Suzie. "I'll be right back," he shouted. He exited the chopper and ran back into the hospital tent.

"Peter!" yelled John as he entered the tent. "We need to do

something."

"John," Peter said calmly, his voice resonating with resignation, "there's nothing we *can* do. Take a glance at the weather map. Do you see the swirling patterns of rain and clouds?" Peter pointed to the weather pattern on his laptop. "Here are the storm predictions, detailing the expected intensity and duration. We expect the storm to arrive in six hours and pass through within 24 hours. The next step in the process is for the search and rescue team to make their way down from Camp 2 and bring him to safety."

"He could be dead by then," shouted John. "That's not good enough!"

Peter raised his eyebrows and shrugged, indicating that he had given his best effort. He then turned his back and was doing something on his laptop computer. John stared at Peter, his eyes filled with a mix of disbelief and anger. Resigned, he finally rushed back to the helicopter.

The rotors of the helicopter were spinning. The pilot prepared to take off, with Jerico sitting opposite him. John climbed back inside next to Suzie.

"Something's not right," whispered Suzie. "Jerico and the pilot are up to something. I'm scared. We need to do something."

John shouted into his headphones, "What the fuck is going

on, Jerico?"

The pilot glanced over at Jerico, who gestured with his index finger, twirling it in the air to signal for takeoff.

John leaned over and kissed Suzie on the lips, feeling a rush of adrenaline before he opened the passenger door. He gracefully leaped out onto the solid ground, slamming the door shut. Locking eyes with John, the pilot shrugged his shoulders, silently mouthing the message, "Your life, your decision." The sound of the rotors intensified. John's eyes followed the helicopter as it ascended into the sky and disappeared down the valley towards Kathmandu.

Chapter Eight

The sensations of dizziness and nausea overcame John as he fought the urge to glance downwards into the gaping crevice. Just an hour before, he'd told Peter he was going to look for Eduardo. Following the doctor's instructions, John securely fastened himself to the safety lines before cautiously stepping onto the narrow aluminum ladder. With its slim width of around 10 inches, there was no space for missteps. He locked his gaze on the other side of the crevice. John took slow, deliberate steps and felt his heart pounding in his chest, afraid of the potential outcome if he were to make even the slightest slip. He thought about Eduardo, and what he needed to do to get to him.

John tried to calm himself, but he kept replaying the image of Peter's stunned reaction when he'd stepped into the hospital tent after the helicopter took off.

"What the hell?" cried Peter.

"I cannot let Eduardo die up there," said John. "I'm going to fetch him and bring him down here."

"That's crazy! You have not adjusted to the altitude," Peter said, noticing John's heavy breathing. "There is a 50 per cent chance that you will experience severe symptoms of altitude sickness. You might die. As you climb higher, that chance steadily increases.

Camp 1 is at 20,000 feet. I suspect you have never been that high before. Am I right?"

"Look Peter, I am going. Are you going to help me or not?"

Peter's eyes narrowed as he fixed a sharp, piercing gaze on John, clearly having a hard time deciding between helping him or not. He watched as John headed out the door, walking away from the tent.

"Wait," John heard Peter shout. "Come back. I'll help you."

John turned around and went back inside. "Thank you, Peter," John sighed.

Peter pulled up a chair for John adjacent to his small desk and sat down. He played the instructional video that detailed the route to Camp 1. It depicted a clearly marked route across the Khumbu Ice field. "One thing you need to know about the route this year is that the icefalls are more unstable than usual," said Peter. "We've experienced a decrease in snowfall compared to previous years. At any moment, the cracks can widen and lead to the ladders collapsing. The ice doctors designed the ladders to allow only one person to climb at a time, but you will pull a 50-pound sled up. During descent, it will weigh 250 pounds. There is a strong possibility that the ladders might not support the additional weight."

In the video, they explained how to secure yourself to the

safety ropes running alongside the ladder, as well as how to safely regain your footing in case of a fall. "You need to hook the medivac sled onto the safety ropes as well," Peter explained. "This year there are five ladders to cross." The video illustrated the proper and safest technique for climbing back onto the ladder.

Peter took John to the storage shed and pulled some items off the shelf. "Here are some crampons to put on the bottom of your boots. The neoprene facemask will keep your skin from freezing." At the back of the storage tent were three medivac sleds on a rack. Peter pulled one down and showed John how to strap it to his body so he could pull it.

"You will probably get altitude sickness," said Peter. "Here are some Diamox and Advil tablets to take now, and some more to take in a few hours." Peter handed John a small baggie, which he stuffed in his pocket. "The storm will hit in six hours. You need to be off the icefall by then. An experienced climber will reach Camp 1 in two hours, but I suspect it will take you four hours. It might be a little faster coming down, but I cannot see you getting back in time." He paused to take a deep breath. "I think you are making a huge mistake. You should not do this."

"I need to do this," said John confidently. "Eduardo and I go back a long way. See you in six hours." He waved goodbye to Peter and headed up the ice field.

One technique John used to overcome his fear of heights was to let his mind drift to other topics. Reliving the moments, he'd spent with Peter had worked. He suddenly realized that he had already passed over the first ladder. He unclipped himself and the sled as he continued upwards to Camp 1—and Eduardo. The route through the icefall was straightforward and easy to track. The sun was radiant, and the sky was a stunning blue hue. John found it difficult to believe that a storm was approaching.

It surprised him how easy it was for him to pull the sled. He thought he would be more breathless than he actually was. Maybe it was his daily 10-kilometre run at home that helped him stay in exceptional shape. Maybe it was his firm resolve to assist his friend that compelled him to push himself to the utmost.

Crossing the second ladder was easier than the first. The gap was narrower, and John discovered that distracting himself with other thoughts reduced the dizziness and nausea. While crossing this ladder, he reminisced about Suzie and the unforgettable week-long sailing trip they took last year, cruising from San Diego to Puerto Vallarta, Mexico. The weather was ideal, with a steady warm breeze that kept the sails full. They spent their days relaxing on the comfortable cushions at the front of the boat, basking in the sun. The dependable boat's auto-helm guided them towards Mexico. Just as the vision of paradise faded from his thoughts, he found himself back on the ice field, continuing his journey.

This is too easy. I have finally conquered my fear of heights. John felt elated. With a surge of confidence, he knew he had the power to overcome any obstacle. He possessed an exceptional mental capacity, which had given a significant advantage in life. *I knew this day would come.*

Halfway across the third ladder, his mind drifted back to a podcast he had listened to in the car on his morning commute a few months ago. Just as the climbers were reaching the summit, a section of cornice collapsed. Two climbers who were not connected to the safety line fell 2,000 feet. They were never recovered. Peering into the frozen chasm of the crevice, dizziness instantly overwhelmed John. He felt faint as nausea washed over him, followed by a rush of bile in his throat. He envisioned the dreadful sensation of falling uncontrollably just before certain demise.

John crouched down, then knelt on the ladder rungs, gripping the edges with his gloved hands, using all the strength he could muster. He gazed at the ladder's end, which was four feet distant. *I can do this.* Despite his unsteadiness, John relied on the medivac sled's handles for support as he stood up. He focused on taking one step at a time. Upon reaching the stable ice, he collapsed onto the snow, gasping for breath. It took at least two minutes for the dizziness to fade and for him to regain his ability to stand.

John glanced at his wristwatch. He had spent three hours on

the icefalls. The time was 3 p.m. He had crossed all five ladders, the last two easier than the ones before. *I must be close to Camp 1*. The weather experts predicted the storm to begin around 6 p.m. just as nightfall was approaching. John noticed that his breathing was becoming more laboured, causing him to take frequent breaks. Feeling a mild headache, one of the initial signs of altitude sickness, he took out his medication from his pocket and swallowed both Diamox and Advil. While walking, he observed the towering ice cliffs that seemed to touch the sky. Now and then, he would hear a rumbling sound when one of the ice cliffs deep within the icefalls collapsed. John desperately hoped that nothing underneath him would collapse.

Upon rounding a corner, a stunning view greeted John. Only 200 metres away was a cluster of red and yellow tents set up on a flat expanse of ice. With a burst of energy, he pushed himself towards Camp 1, feeling his muscles surge with strength. As a wave of elation swept through his body; his hopes were renewed. He had done it, and a sense of accomplishment washed over John. The prospect of returning appeared less daunting to him, reasoning that it would involve a downhill journey. Now he had to focus on finding Eduardo.

Confidence filled John as he anticipated completing the task before the storm arrived. The closer he got to the tents, the more he noticed the eerie silence. Something was off. The camp was completely quiet, devoid of any signs of life or movement, unless the climbers were taking shelter in their tents. None of the stoves emitted a wisp of smoke. The camp, with its empty tents and silent atmosphere, gave the impression of being completely deserted.

John went up to the first tent and shouted, "Hello? Anyone there?" The silence that followed his response was deafening. The sound of John's voice reverberated through the frozen landscape, bouncing off the ice and rock formations, creating a mesmerizing echo. Using both hands, he pulled back the flaps of the tent, revealing the interior. The area had no occupants or belongings, rendering it void of any signs of life. The absence of even a sleeping bag and a backpack was noticeable. He walked over to the adjacent tent, unzipped it, and peered inside. It was empty as well. It appeared that no one was occupying any of the 20 tents scattered across the ice field. John approached the last one with trepidation. Unzipping the front flap, he took a glimpse inside.

The outline of a body, snugly wrapped in a polar sleeping bag, occupied one side of the tent. The tight string of the sleeping bag distorted the facial features. John crawled into the tent and partially unzipped the sleeping bag to check for a carotid pulse. A strong one was present. Eduardo's unique facial characteristics, coupled with a week's worth of beard growth, made him easily identifiable. John noticed that his breathing was slow and shallow.

He shook his friend. "Eduardo, are you awake?" John shook him once more, and he noticed a pained expression appear on Eduardo's face. His eyes fluttered open. The dilated pupils darted around in a bewildered and erratic manner as he attempted to rise. He let out a piercing scream before collapsing onto the ground. Eduardo appeared to calm down after that. After a moment, he gazed at John with sorrowful eyes, realizing it was his friend.

"I've come to take you to safety," said John.

Eduardo looked at John and shook his head. "You need to get away from here," he whispered. "Someone tried to kill me."

Chapter Nine

When the helicopter left base camp without John, Suzie stared in disbelief as she watched him look up at them as they flew away. Her pulse was racing, and the shortness of breath she had experienced at base camp appeared to worsen. She was hyperventilating. She could feel panic take over her body.

"You need to go back and pick him up!" Suzie shouted into the headphones.

When there was no response, she banged her hand on the pilot's shoulder, which startled him. The helicopter abruptly veered to the right and then sharply swung back to the left as he made a quick steering correction. "Go back and get him!" she screamed. Suzie repeatedly struck his shoulder, causing the helicopter to bounce with each hit. She felt a hand grab her wrist, preventing her from giving another blow to the pilot.

"Stop that before we crash!" shouted Jerico. "We are not going back!" He pushed Suzie back in her seat.

Tears streamed down Suzie's face as she cried in frustration. "Please, Jerico," she pleaded. "Go back and get him. He is going to die. He has not acclimatized."

"Suzie," said Jerico, "that was his choice to jump out of the helicopter before we took off. Going back to get him would be pointless because he wouldn't come. By now you should know that about him. The lack of fuel would leave us stranded on the mountain without a way to return. Both you and Mathew would be in grave danger.

"I don't care!" cried Suzie. "Go back and get him!"

Jerico just shook his head and turned away, looking through the helicopter's front window. Suzie wept the entire journey back to Kathmandu, with Mathew trying to console her. Her tears had dried by the time they arrived. An overwhelming rage soon engulfed the frustration she felt. Exiting the helicopter, she hurriedly made her way to the flight-booking counter.

She approached the attendant, a Nepali woman who looked to be in her forties. "I need a helicopter to take me to the base camp," said Suzie. "I don't care what it costs. I need it now. Those assholes left my husband stranded there. I need to get him back."

The attendant looked at Suzie's red eyes. "Honey," she said, "there is a storm coming. We have grounded all the choppers for the next 24 hours. It is not safe to go."

Suzie stared at her with a blank expression. "The skies are bright blue. Surely the forecast is wrong. John is up there on the mountain alone. He has not acclimatized. He could die. Please help me!"

The attendant looked at her warmly. "Honey, trust me. He will be fine," she said kindly. "Many climbers fly to base camp with us without acclimatizing and they do just fine. The storm will be over tomorrow at this time. Come back then and I'll see what I can do to get you up there."

Suzie's eyes welled up once more. Before long, tears streamed down her face. "Please, please. I can't just leave him up there. You need to help me."

The attendant as she wrote her cell phone number on a yellow sticky and pasted it on the glass wall that separated them.

"Thank you," said Suzie. She turned around and walked out the door.

Jerico and Mathew stood side by side, patiently waiting by the bustling taxi stand. "Let's go," said Jerico.

"Jerico, you can go and fuck yourself!" Suzie shouted. She hopped in the first taxi and instructed the driver to take her to the hotel. She needed to come up with a plan.

Suzie slammed down the phone, then stared at it. The phone recording at the Canadian embassy in Kathmandu instructed her to leave a message. She had already left four other messages in the past hour, and this was the fifth one. At 3 p.m. on a weekday, there should be someone there. Suzie grabbed her cell phone and headed to the lobby.

"I need a taxi to take me to the Canadian embassy," said Suzie. The concierge bowed his head graciously and gestured with his hand for her to follow him. On the circular stone driveway, a line of white X-press EV taxis from the Tata car company in India sat silently, ready to transport passengers. In their compact cars, the drivers relaxed with the front doors wide open, enjoying the fresh breeze. Further back in line, they leaned against the hoods, smoking, the smell lingering in the air. The concierge opened the rear door of the first one. Suzie got inside and then he closed the door. He uttered something to the driver, who nodded in understanding and drove towards the main road, inching along in the traffic congestion. Suzie could sense her frustration mounting. She was overwhelmed by the events of the past few hours.

The taxi dropped Suzie off in front of the Canadian embassy. It was in an old white stucco building with large brown wooden doors. She pressed the doorbell and waited. There was no answer. Suzie banged on the door with her fists. There was still no answer. It was then she noticed a sign pasted to the window: The Canadian Consulate is open 10:30–13:30 Monday to Friday. To make an appointment, email kathmandu@international.gc.ca.

Suzie sat on the steps of the consulate, trying to think of her next move. The time in Canada was 5:00 a.m. She would need to wait another four hours before she could call the Canadian Consulate in Ottawa. By then it would be 7:15 p.m. in Kathmandu. Too dark for a helicopter to fly. There was little they could do to help. She looked at her phone and did a Google search on how to get to base camp from Kathmandu. The best option would be to take a flight to Lukla, the same place she had visited earlier in the day for refuelling the helicopter. The duration of the trek from there to base camp was 13 days. This situation was quickly becoming a terrible nightmare.

She used Google Maps to locate walking directions to the hotel. It would take 30 minutes; the same time the taxi took. As Suzie strode quickly, she hoped she could think of something that would help John. Nothing came to her mind. She arrived at the hotel, her mind racing. The only solution she could think of was reaching out to her brother, Marco, for guidance. It was 5:30 a.m. in Toronto. She knew he would be awake.

"Marco," she said when he answered. "I need your help." He listened as Suzie told him what had happened at the base camp. "I think there is more going on here than what I have told you," she continued. "The mere presence of Jerico and Peter sends a shiver through me. I can see the insincerity etched on their faces every time we have a conversation."

"While John can be impulsive, he is a quick thinker and will navigate his way through this," said Marco. "The thing that's really bothering me is your description of the events involving Jerico and Peter. I'd like to know more about what is going on between them. It's possible that you are at risk, so make sure to keep your distance from them. Let me think about this, and I'll call you back in a while."

As the older sibling, Marco assumed the responsibility of being Suzie's protector, safeguarding her from any harm or danger. During their time living in Colombia, he'd actively taken part in the revolutionary army known as the FARC. Marco had successfully engaged in negotiations with the government, resulting in a lasting peace agreement that still stands to this day. The revolutionary group had factions with differing levels of radicalism, and it was the more extreme elements who accused him of being a traitor.

When they threatened to kill him, Marco fled to Canada as a refugee. He had been living there for the past 10 years. While he worked as a mechanic in an auto shop, his abilities extended well beyond the scope of his job. With his ability to read people and analyze their body language, he had a knack for anticipating their next move. It was what kept him alive throughout those challenging times in Colombia.

As Suzie was thinking about her brother, there was a knock on her door. She peered through the peephole and saw Mathew's familiar face staring back at her. She opened the door and let him in.

"There has been an avalanche at base camp."

Chapter Ten

"Where are they now?" asked Jerico. Sitting in his hotel suite in Kathmandu, he could hear the muffled sounds of the bustling city outside. He lounged on the comfortable sofa, warmed by the crackling fire. In his hand, he held a glass of Scotch on the rocks, the ice clinking softly with each sip. Jerico needed to take control of the situation. John's unexpected leap from the helicopter left everyone stunned, but as he contemplated the situation, he realized it could work to his benefit.

"I see John getting prepared to cross the fifth ladder near Camp 1," said Peter.

"Can you put your satellite phone on speaker?" asked Jerico.

"Will do. I'm looking through the telescope at a figure struggling to pull the medivac sled across the treacherous Khumbu Icefall. As clear as day, I can see John carefully connect himself to the safety lines. Now he's attaching the medivac sled. This telescope gives me exceptional resolution," he said, almost offering a play-by-play of the action. "I can observe every detail on his face, revealing what looks like an unwavering determination! He seems cautious, though, as he crosses the ladder. Oh… I see John unclipping the sled from the safety line and then himself. He is on his downward trek to the next ladder. Wait! He's pulling the sled containing Eduardo."

"So they have crossed the ladder now?" asked Jerico.

"Yep. On the way to the next one."

"OK, thanks," said Jerico. "Let me know when they cross the last ladder just above the base camp."

"Will do," said Peter. "That should be in about two hours from now if they move quickly."

Jerico hung up and took another sip of his whisky. A few nights ago, a man named Sergio Leone had approached him in the hotel bar to discuss his latest business venture. But Jerico's mind was on the long-legged blond woman seated next to him. He detected a German accent when she told him she was planning to go backpacking and gain some life experience travelling before settling down. She'd finished a business degree in Munich and was up for an adventure.

Jerico saw his opportunity. He pointed to a sharply dressed man who was sitting down at the bar. "Do you know that fellow?" he asked. She turned to her left, squinting in the darkness. Jerico slipped some powdered Rohypnol into her gin fizz and stirred it with the swizzle stick.

"Nope," she said. "Never seen him in here before."

Jerico couldn't help but smile as she took a big gulp of her cocktail. *It's going to be a good night*, he thought. Within the next three minutes, his blond quarry started slurring her speech. She had a faraway look in her eyes. In five more minutes, he would escort her out of the bar and take her to his hotel room. She wouldn't remember a thing when she woke up in her own room the following morning.

"We need to talk." The voice came from a tall, thin man standing beside him. In his late fifties, he had a distinguished appearance, with a full head of salt and pepper hair. His intense blue eyes seemed to pierce through Jerico's soul.

Jerico looked up at him with a startled expression. Without uttering a word, the man retrieved his cell phone and played a video where Jerico had pointed at something. A second later, the screen displayed a clear image of him adding a white powder to the woman's drink.

"I need you to come with me," said the man, as he put the cell phone into his jacket pocket. He turned around, walked out of the bar and into the hotel lobby.

At first, Jerico was not sure what to do. He stood up and stole a glance at his prospective date, who had tilted her head against the wall and seemed to have drifted off to sleep. *She will have to wait,* he thought. This man might be trouble. He needed to find out what he wanted. Jerico walked out of the bar and sat beside the tall man in the hotel lobby.

"We need to go somewhere private," said the tall man. "Let's go to my room."

"Not a chance," said Jerico. "We talk here or not at all."

They were the only ones in the hotel lobby, except for the desk clerk at the reception desk, but he was out of earshot. The tall man's gaze shifted upward to the ceiling. The lobby had cameras positioned in the corners, but there were none directly above. Despite the absence of visible microphones, he cautiously pulled out his cell phone and launched a microphone-jamming app for added security.

"Have it your way," he said.

"What do you want from me?" asked Jerico.

"My name is Sergio Leone. I represent the Brothers of Italy. We're the right-wing populist party in Italy," he said. "Now listen carefully. The owner of Italy's largest private company, Gianni Rattazzi senior, is dying. His only son, Eduardo Rattazzi, is to inherit the business. After converting to the Shia Muslim faith, we worry Eduardo will dismantle the company and send all the profits to support those terrorist organizations in Iran. This would be a disaster for our political future."

Jerico looked at him incredulously. "What the fuck has any of this to do with me?" he said in a loud voice.

"You are going to see to it that Eduardo Rattazzi perishes on Everest," Sergio said calmly.

"You are out of your mind!"

Without faltering, Sergio calmly directed his gaze forward and uttered, "Your participation in the $5 million black heroin racket is no secret to us. If you want to keep that going, you will do as I ask. I doubt you want the video I filmed spread across social media."

Jerico went red in the face and could feel his heart pumping. Fuelled by adrenaline, he instinctively attacked, attempting to reach Sergio with a sudden lunge. Sergio was ready. While adeptly avoiding the attack, he landed a powerful blow by striking both of his hands against Jerico's ears. He heard a loud popping sound, followed by severe pain in both ears. In agony, Jerico collapsed to the ground, whimpering softly and clutching his ears.

Jerico slowly got up and sat down next to Sergio. "What do you want me to do?" Jerico asked. The constant ringing in his ears, along with the intense pain it caused, completely quelled any notions he had of retaliating.

That was a few days ago. Jerico was going over Sergio's explicit instructions in his head when his phone rang.

"They are coming over the last bridge now."

It was Peter, calling on his satellite phone. "OK," said Jerico. "Thanks. You know what you have to do," He hung up without saying goodbye.

Jerico logged onto his computer and opened the app that controlled the drone. He started the motor and remotely flew it up the Khumbu Icefalls. The image on the screen was clear. He saw a figure pulling a medivac sled. The man looked up. John. The camera resolution was good, but Jerico couldn't clearly see who was on the sled. The drone was having some difficulty because of the powerful gusts that had arrived in advance of the storm.

They were almost in position, under the serac, a 60-foot block of ice.

Chapter Eleven

"I am not leaving this mountain without you," said John, determination etched on his face. Eduardo, still wrapped up in the sleeping bag at Camp 1, glanced up, shaking his head.

"That means both of us are going to die," he said grimly. "I think they tried to poison me."

"Why do you think that?"

Eduardo sighed. "They've done it before."

"What! You've been poisoned before?" John looked at Eduardo incredulously. *Is he mentally incapacitated? High-altitude cerebral edema, perhaps?*

"No, no. Not me." Eduardo paused as if it were a painful memory. "There is a woman who told me the story of her father getting poisoned. It was when I was just a boy in Turin, Italy, growing up. The leader of the automobile union was none other than her father. He was tirelessly organizing a strike, fighting for fair wages that would provide a decent living for the workers. She told me she thought my father was to blame for her father's death."

John, captivated by the story, shook his head as if to clear his thoughts. *I need to get him out of here. This story has nothing to do with his seizure. He is clearly confused.*

John smiled at his friend as he lay in the tent. "Let me look at your arm," he said. John unzipped the sleeping bag and sat Eduardo up. "I need to take your jacket and shirt off to look at it."

John delicately took off the items. There was a slight bend in Eduardo's right arm, and it was at an unnatural angle. There was swelling along the radius, indicating an injury. Upon further examination, John could feel a fracture in the mid-portion of the bone. Eduardo's face contorted in agony as John delicately ran his fingers along the surface of the bone.

"Before I move you, I need to stabilize the fracture," said John. "I'll be right back."

John crawled out of the tent and looked for something to splint the fractured arm. There was an aluminum walking stick left behind in one tent that might work. He bent it in half. Himalayan prayer flags attached to a string between two tents danced and fluttered in the gentle breeze. According to what John had read, blue represented the vastness of the sky, yellow symbolized the grounding of the earth, white embodied the gentle breezes of wind and air, red represented the fierce power of fire, and green represented the calming presence of water. John, reflecting on his love of sailing, chose a green prayer flag and a white one to secure the aluminum splint for stabilizing Eduardo's broken bone. When he descended with Eduardo, he hoped that the prayer flags would carry his wishes for good fortune.

John crawled back into Eduardo's tent. The bent aluminum pole served as an ideal splint, effectively immobilizing the fracture and preventing any further movement. John used the prayer flags to tie the aluminum pole halves in place. He made a sling out of Eduardo's shirt to further stabilize the fracture and prevent movement.

"Do you think you can walk?" asked John.

"I do not have any boots," said Eduardo. "They must have taken them."

"Eduardo, what the hell is going on?" asked John. Concern filled John's eyes as he looked at his friend.

Eduardo gazed up at John and sighed. "It's a long story. If we get out of here alive, I'll tell you. In the meantime, let's get moving."

John helped Eduardo onto the sled and placed him under the thermal survival emergency blanket. Using the red canvas of the medivac sled, he cocooned him, strapping him firmly in place with the black safety straps. Eduardo's smiling face poked out of the back end of the sled. "Are you sure you want to do this?" he asked. "You might get yourself in a heap of trouble helping me."

John smiled. "It's too late now. I've got you tied up. You're coming with me!"

Eduardo laughed. "Your life, your decision."

"That's what the helicopter pilot seemed to tell me when I jumped out at base camp," said John. "Up to this point, this impulsive strategy has proven to be successful for me."

With determination in his eyes, John started hauling the heavy sled towards base camp, the sound of the dragging echoing through the frozen icefall. Going downhill, the heavy sled became easier to pull as John descended the slope, making sure not to lose control. The sturdy sled handles provided him with stability as he navigated the slippery terrain. As he neared the first of five ladders, a wave of dizziness washed over him at the mere thought of crossing them. As his fear of heights consumed him, he could feel his chest constricting with tension.

"I have a confession," said John as he turned to Eduardo. "I am terrified of heights. The only way I made it to you is by immersing myself in an alternate reality, pretending I was somewhere else."

"Just my luck," said Eduardo. "Getting pulled to my death by a psycho. Do you want me to sing? I learned Puccini's 'Nessun Dorma' as a child. Whenever I get a little anxious, I belt out a few verses. I can guarantee it will distract you and prevent you from falling into the crevice."

With that, he started in a deep baritone, belting out the opera in a loud voice. John's laughter echoed through the air as he secured himself and the sled onto the safety lines. The thought of a mountain climber belting out opera tunes while being towed on a sled through the snowy Himalayas struck him as utterly absurd. Before he thought any more about his fear of heights, he was across the ladder bridge. As John unclipped the safety lines, Eduardo had become slightly breathless from the singing at such a high altitude and abruptly stopped.

"You made it across!" said Eduardo. "How was my opera rendition?

"I am surprised it was so good," John said. "I have fond memories of you from our time in the drama club in school, where you were always the one who loved to ham it up on stage. While I quit to spend more time in the beach-rescue activities, you became the star in the year end drama production... I can't even remember what it was."

"The drama coach asked you to leave," Eduardo said, "because of your poor acting abilities, if I remember correctly."

"I can't deny that," John deadpanned. "Let's get a move on."

John began pulling the sled towards base camp. He and Eduardo repeated the same routine for every bridge. The singing was a helpful distraction. They had just passed the last bridge when John felt the gust of wind that seemed to come out of nowhere with an icy blast. Over the past hour, dark clouds had replaced the bright, sunny blue sky.

This must be the beginning of the storm, thought John. He could see the base camp from where he was standing. It couldn't be more than half an hour away at the rate they were descending. A whirring noise came from above as John watched a drone fly overhead. *Someone's coming to see if we are OK,* he thought. John waved and gave a thumbs up sign to the passing drone. They were almost back at the base camp.

John had noticed a headache on the front of his head. It had been getting worse over the past hour, so he swallowed another Advil and Diamox. The headache persisted as a throbbing ache, but now it was affecting his vision. The path seemed to be wavy when he knew it was straight. John knew this was high- altitude sickness and the only cure was to get to a lower elevation. They were passing under a 60-foot serac. There was a storm a few days ago and John could see a large precipice of overhanging snow. He was fatiguing, but the proximity of the base camp kept him motivated to keep going.

John turned around to check on his friend. Eduardo had stopped singing now they were past the bridge.

"Almost home!" shouted John above the roar of the wind. "One last push to get us…"

Just as he was speaking, a loud blast broke the silence, followed by a deep riveting crack from the serac. In a quick glance, John observed the ridge of ice splitting apart.

"Avalanche!" shouted Eduardo from the sled. "Run, run! Go John!"

In a flash, John jolted forward with the speed and intensity of a lightning bolt. His heart pounded as adrenaline coursed through his body. As they were going downhill, the sled provided momentum and propelled him forward. With his arms securely strapped to the handles, he accelerated with the sled's speed. The sound of the avalanche was deafening as the ice crashed behind him. A roar resembling the thunder of 100 jet plane engines reverberated through the icefalls. To the left, he saw the sea of ice and snow barrel towards base camp. *Somehow, the massive avalanche is missing us.* At that very moment, a massive block of ice, resembling a breadbox in size, crashed into John's back. He lost his balance. Like a bowling pin that had been knocked down with force, his body rolled and flipped uncontrollably. He could feel soft snow bounce him around as his speed seemed to increase.

The heart-pounding ordeal finally came to an end, and he felt himself come to a sudden stop, his body still trembling with fear. John's arms were bound up in the straps of the sled handle. He couldn't move. The pain in his head was unbearable, as if his skull was being shattered into pieces. All he could do was wiggle his head and neck, unable to move any other part of his body. Confusion clouded his mind as he struggled to determine his orientation, unsure if he was facing up or down. A deep darkness shrouded everything. As his head broke through the snowpack, he could feel the sharp chill of the winter air against his skin through his neoprene face cover.

He gasped for air.

The wind was relentless, yet he persisted in inhaling deeply, determined to steady his racing heart. He couldn't seem to get enough air into his lungs. As soon as he realized he was still alive, despite his inability to move, his immediate thought was of Eduardo. He yelled with all his might, desperately calling out, "Eduardo! Eduardo!"

He listened. All he could hear were the gusts of wind and snow.

Chapter Twelve

"What did you see?" asked Jerico.

"The colossal serac collapsed as they were passing underneath," said Peter. The satellite phone was on speaker as he peered through the telescope. "It's hard to see now because it is getting dark, and the storm just blew in. It's a whiteout. I see nothing. We need to send a team up on the icefall to see if they are alive…" he said, trailing off. "Although there is no way they could have survived that mass of ice that crashed into them."

"You'll do nothing of the sort," shouted Jerico. "No one must know they were there."

"That's crazy! The avalanche buried some tents at the far end of base camp. A rescue team is getting mobilized to see if anyone there got injured. John and Eduardo are less that half an hour away. It would be nothing for them to extend the search."

"You are to say nothing about them to the rescue team," replied Jerico. "That was the deal."

Peter thought about the picture of his parents at their Toronto home Jerico had shown him. The smile on his mother's face spoke volumes of the love they had for each other. *What have I got myself into? What the hell have I done to John and Eduardo?* Peter remained quiet, not knowing what to say to Jerico. He hung up the phone without saying goodbye. He put his head in his hands as despondency set in. His parents would be so disappointed in him if they ever found out he was involved in the death of innocent people.

Peter knew what he had to do.

He zipped up his Gore-Tex jacket and pulled on his down-filled snow pants and parka, preparing to brave the cold. He put on his headlamp over his balaclava. The mittens would keep his hands warm up to minus 40°C. He could rely on the crampons equipped on the snow boots to prevent him from losing his footing on the icy terrain. He would embark on the challenging journey up the Khumbu Icefalls, carefully navigating the slick terrain.

Peter went to the storage shed to select an ice axe. This would be an essential piece of equipment to prevent him from falling into the concealed crevasse beneath the snowy surface. The visibility was perhaps two feet as the wind blew the snow horizontally. Powerful gusts funnelled up the valley. He knew the winds would hamper his progress. The Garmin Mountain watch he wore on his right wrist told him that the temperature with the wind chill was minus 50°C.

Peter opened the door to the storage shed and turned on the light. Asleep on a canvas sack was Pesang, the Sherpa who delivered the black heroin to Jerico a few weeks ago. He bolted upright upon hearing the roar of the wind and feeling the icy blast come through the door.

"What the hell are you doing here?" asked Peter.

Pesang's eyes locked on Peter, his brow furrowing as he contemplated his next words. "The boss was to pick this up later this week." He pointed to the canvas sack. "The storm blew in so quickly, I didn't have time to get home, so I am hunkering down here until it blows over. You look like you're heading out somewhere." He paused as he watched Peter select an ice axe from the shelf. "That's not a good idea. You might not come back. With all the time you have spent up here, I would assume you would know better."

"You might not have heard, but there was an avalanche. Some climbers got stuck in it coming back from Camp 1. The rescue crew is busy digging out some tents further up in the base camp, so they can't help. I'm going to search for them. Can you come with me?"

Without missing a beat, Pesang replied, "No fucking way. That is suicide. If I went with you, it would only add to the death toll. It's madness to go out in this!" Pesang positioned himself on the canvas bag and faced away from Peter to signal he was done with talking.

Peter shrugged his shoulders and opened the door. Another icy blast of snow pellets and wind greeted him. Knowing he was risking his life, he began his trek to search for Eduardo and John. To stay indoors, sheltered from the storm, was not something he could contemplate when he could help someone trapped on the mountain. The weight of guilt for his involvement in the massacre was so heavy that the idea of his own death seemed like a welcome release.

Large chunks of ice and snow had transformed the once well-travelled pathway to Camp 1 into an icy obstacle course. Peter used his GPS to travel on the route where the path should have been. Some chunks of ice were the size of houses, which made the travelling slow. Sometimes he met a wall of ice and had to backtrack. There were areas covered in soft snow from the avalanche. Peter walked with his ice axe to poke into the powder before he took a step to avoid falling into a snow-covered crevice. He carried ropes and grommets strapped to his back in case he fell into one. This was not the night to be on the mountain by himself. There was no one who could help him if he got into trouble.

Guilt continued to wash over Peter, consuming him as he thought about what had happened to John and Eduardo. While he wasn't the one responsible for pushing the detonator, a sinking feeling should have alerted him to the impending disaster. He didn't question Jerico when he positioned the drone outside of the Everest ER as Jerico instructed. He admonished himself for not demanding an explanation. *How was I to know he would use it to blow up a serac and cause a devastating avalanche?*

Helping those in need of medical attention became the purpose of his life. To be the one providing their position on the mountain so someone else could harm them was just as bad as pushing the button himself. As he made his way up the treacherous Khumbu Icefall in the dark and cold, Peter's concern for his own safety seemed to fade away, driven solely by the determination to find the two men.

After about an hour, his GPS showed the path he travelled had been a circle. He was only about a mile from base camp, a distance he would normally travel in 15 minutes. He realized it was foolish to look for them in these terrible conditions. With his mind clouded by guilt and responsibility, he had not been thinking clearly when he left. Making his way through the wreckage caused by the avalanche, Peter forcefully drove the tip of his ice axe into the snowy terrain. The end of the object penetrated deeply into the soft snow, suggesting a potential crevasse beneath it.

A gust of wind pushed him headfirst into the soft snow. Peter felt himself falling into the crevice. At first, it felt like slow motion, but then he reacted quickly, using the axe to dig into the ice wall and stopping his fall into the crevasse just a few feet from the top. He breathed a sigh of relief. The light from his powerful headlamp shone inside the icy maw, showing the jagged walls to the bottom several stories below.

Looking upwards, Peter knew he had only to climb two feet to reach the top and pull himself out. Holding the ice axe with both hands, he gripped the wall with his crampons, gaining 12 inches closer to the top. The next step would be more difficult. He had to pull out the ice axe and plant it higher on the wall of ice. Confirming that his feet were well dug in, he took a deep breath and wrenched on the ice axe. He released it smoothly. *Phew*, he exhaled. When he went to plant it higher into the wall, he lost his grip. The tool flew out of his hands. He felt his body fall backwards into the crevasse. Bouncing off the walls slowed his descent, so when he landed on his back at the bottom seconds later, he lay there assessing how much damage he had done.

Peter breathed slowly as he wiggled his toes, then moved his legs and arms. He anticipated having bruises, but he remained confident that no bones had broken. To his surprise, his headlight was still working and casting a warm glow up the 30-foot crevice of glistening ice. It was relatively small, but he needed to get out before the crevice moved and crushed him. Peter stood up and assessed his situation. As part of the base camp's requirements, he had practised climbing out of a crevasse during the mountain rescue training exercises that all faculty members were required to complete.

The ice axe had landed a few feet away from him. Peter picked it up. The walls of the crevasse were steep, but there were ledges where he could get a handhold. With the crampons on his boots providing traction, he could straddle the narrow crevasse and make his way up. The ice axe helped by getting some vertical purchase so he could pull himself higher. Even though it was freezing, he could sense the sweat trickling down his body beneath his winter attire.

As Peter inched up to the summit of the crevasse, the walls became slightly less steep, levelling out at a 45-degree angle. He figured he could crawl by using the ice axe to pull himself up to the edge. *Just a little more*, he promised himself. At the top, he rolled onto his back to catch his breath. Exhausted, he lay there in the howling wind for about 10 minutes before he got up. The conditions had become worse. He knew he needed to get back to base camp.

Despite the 30-foot fall, the handheld GPS miraculously continued to function. It showed him the way to get back to base camp. Following the previous route seemed pointless, as Peter had gone in circles. The map, however, showed a direct path, albeit one that required manoeuvring around large chunks of ice.

After trudging along for about half an hour, he suddenly stumbled over something in his path. With a quick reflex, he steadied himself before losing his balance. His eyes shifted downwards, and he focused his attention on his feet. The snow had concealed most of it, but a red edge peeked through. Peter brushed off the snow. It was the medivac sled he'd given to John.

With a rush of excitement, he swiftly flipped the sled over and eagerly loosened the ties. The sled was empty. Peter moved his light in circular patterns, scanning for the two men, but all he witnessed was the snow swirling around him. "John!" he shouted.

The sounds of the wind howling were like that of someone screaming for help. "John! Eduardo!" he repeated. He cocked his ear towards the wind, hoping to discern a voice through its roar. Nothing came that sounded human. With the position marked on the GPS so he could return the following day when the storm subsided, he pressed on towards base camp.

Chapter Thirteen

As John realized he could get enough air, his breathing seemed to calm and become steady. If it weren't for the throbbing headache, he would have only been bothered by the minor bruises on his limbs. He could move his arms and legs only enough to be certain there were no broken bones. Yet he remained trapped beneath the weight of the avalanche. His eyes darted around but saw nothing in the pitch blackness.

He gradually breathed at a slower pace. Overwhelmed by fatigue, John closed his eyes. A wave of exhaustion swept through his body, leaving him completely defeated. The feeling of his body relaxing gradually enveloped him, bringing a sense of calm and ease. While the idea of never waking up briefly crossed his mind, he ultimately succumbed to the temptation of descending into that deep hole of comfort and rest.

John opened his eyes. He woke up disoriented, not knowing how much time had passed since he lost consciousness. Something shook his body, causing a shiver to run down his spine. Now that his right arm was no longer restrained, he swiftly used it to release his left arm from its confinement. As he swept the snow off his legs, he collided with a solid object, jolting his arm.

"John!" screamed the voice, barely audible above the gusts of wind. *Was it Peter?*

"Peter!?" screamed John. He felt confused, at first not sure where he was. Despite his attempt to stand, John quickly lost his balance, and his legs crumpled underneath him. He tried to stand again. Like two twigs bent in the wind, his legs would not support him. He lay in the snow, feeling the ground spinning. *What the hell is going on? I keep falling over.* John remained on his back and felt someone crawl up to him. He touched the familiar face of his friend.

"Eduardo, it's you. Thank God you're OK. I cannot stand up."

"You have HACE," he shouted in John's ear. "High-altitude cerebral edema. Falling over is one of the early symptoms. We need to get you to base camp, then fly you to Kathmandu by helicopter."

"I feel disorientated," said John. "I can't tell what is up or down."

"Let me help you up. In a minute or two, you should be able to stand on your own."

John extended his arm upwards to grasp Eduardo's hand. With a shaky stance, he leaned against his friend, clutching tightly to his body, desperately trying to maintain his balance. John tried to open his eyes wide to discern the horizon. He hoped that would help him keep his balance. All he saw was blackness. With each passing moment, John's assurance in his ability to stay upright increased. In a hesitant manner, he slowly released his grip on Eduardo. Despite feeling a bit shaky, he started to regain his sense of balance.

"I don't think I can pull you in the sled," shouted John. "The ground is too uneven."

"We can tie a rope around ourselves," said Eduardo, directly into John's ear. "In case either of us falls, the other can quickly locate and assist."

"You don't have any shoes. How are you going to walk?" John strained his eyes to catch a glimpse of Eduardo's feet, but the swirling snow and darkness obscured his view.

"I used my mittens to wrap around my feet. Let's go. We'll head downwards until we hit the edge of the icefalls, then we'll walk along the rocks until we reach the base camp." Eduardo's voice battled against the roaring wind as he shouted, but John pieced together enough words to feel confident in his understanding of the plan.

Eduardo led the way. The Khumbu Icefall gradually drifted in a downward fashion. The location where the icefall and the rocky terrain intersected is precisely where the base camp was situated. John walked behind Eduardo as he poked the end of the ice axe he'd retrieved from the medivac sled into the snow before he made each step. He used his good arm while the broken arm remained wrapped up in the sling tight against his chest. This slowed them down, but John understood this was necessary to avoid falling into a crevasse. On their downward climb, when they encountered large chunks of ice, they would trudge around them but always using gravity to guide them towards the bottom of the icefalls. It was pitch black, and the wind continued its howling racket, with ice blasts of snow pummelling into their face guards. It was difficult for John to keep his balance. Yet after every time he fell over, Eduardo would patiently help him up. His headache was unbearable, but he knew they had no choice but to press on.

John toppled over again, but this time he landed on hard rocks. A sharp pain reverberated from his right hip where he landed. *Just another bruise to add to the list.* He tried to stand up but lost his balance and tumbled down again, but this time he did not hurt himself. They were at the end of the icefall, and John knew they had to follow the edge to get to base camp. The rocks were uneven, so the travel would be rough. Eduardo helped John stand.

"I think you have snow blindness," said Eduardo. "I can see the rocks, though, so I want you to hold on to my jacket. It will help you keep your balance while we walk down the last bit. We're almost there. Hold on tight. We are going to make it!"

John gripped the back of Eduardo's jacket. It was much

easier walking on the rocks than on the snow. Every time he stumbled, Eduardo would brace himself so John could stay upright. The rocks were uneven, and John took each step tentatively, to be sure of solid ground. Eduardo seemed to have a strong sense of where the best path lay, so although John couldn't see the ground, he could move forward as his confidence built.

The ground appeared to flatten, and John could feel Eduardo quicken his pace. With his fingers clenched tightly around Eduardo's jacket, John strained to keep his eyes focused straight ahead, even though the object in his grasp remained invisible. He continued to put one foot in front of the other, feeling the rough terrain beneath his boots and relying on Eduardo's guidance to lead him to safety. Suddenly, Eduardo came to a halt. John collided with him and nearly lost his balance. John felt the warmth of the air enveloping the exposed skin above his eyebrows. Eduardo led him into a room and carefully seated him in a chair. For the first time since leaving base camp to search for his friend, John felt secure.

With the wind's howl fading to a gentle murmur, after Eduardo closed the door, he could finally hear his voice clearly. "We made it to Everest ER," said Eduardo. "But no one is here."

"I can't see anything."

Eduardo pulled off John's neoprene balaclava. "Let's give it a minute," said Eduardo. "Your eyelashes have frozen shut."

Despite his efforts, John's eyes remained closed. Finally, he resorted to gently pinching his eyelashes with his fingertips, causing the ice to melt and allowing him to open them. He noticed that there was a distinct yellow halo surrounding the objects in the room.

Eduardo's face, filled with concern, leaned towards him. "How are you feeling?" he asked.

John looked around the room. He recognized they were in the Everest ER. His headache was pounding, but he breathed an enormous sigh of relief. "I'm a lot better now that we are out of the storm, but I feel like an axe is splitting my head open. How are your feet?"

"I think they're frozen."

"Let me have a look at them."

John stood up, but immediately felt dizzy. Before he fell over again, he managed to catch himself and sit down. Eduardo sat in a chair in front of John and removed the mittens from his feet. John could see that the four small toes on each foot had frozen white. The tips of the big toes were white and also frozen, but the rest of them were pink. "Eduardo," said John. "Fill up two of those basins on the shelf with lukewarm water. We need to immerse your feet to thaw your toes to slowly get the circulation back."

With a slight limp, Eduardo exerted effort as he made his

way to the shelf, where he successfully filled the basins by operating a foot pump connected to a tap. Placing the basins on the floor, he immersed both feet into the water.

"As the circulation restores, there will be an intense itchiness," said John. "You must not touch the skin. After a few minutes, severe pain will replace the itchiness. If the toes survive, you'll have painful blisters for the next few days. I had a lot of experience with frozen digits during a rotation when I was in medical school in the far north of Canada during a particularly cold winter."

Eduardo glanced at his frozen toes. "They are getting itchy now," he said. His face grimaced as the discomfort progressed.

"That's good," said John. "It means we got to them in time, and you are less likely to get gangrene."

With a startled expression, Eduardo turned his gaze towards John, clearly affected by the unexpected nature of his remarks. "That would mean the end of my climbing career." He turned to look at his toes again. "But perhaps that wouldn't be such a bad thing after all," he said wistfully.

"Eduardo, what the hell happened up on the mountain?"

Eduardo's voice grew softer, and he became quiet, lost in his thoughts. As he raised his gaze to meet John's, a deep sense of sadness filled his eyes, and he opened his mouth to speak. "I was…" An icy blast of cold air filled the room as the clinic door burst open.

It was Peter. With the wind roaring, he shouted while shutting the door to make himself heard. "Thank God you two are OK."

Chapter Fourteen

Jerico watched the news with satisfaction. "An avalanche in the Khumbu Icefalls took out at least five tents at Mount Everest Base Camp," said the serious news anchor on CNN. "The strong winds and blizzard conditions have made it difficult to launch a rescue operation."

The video image flipped to a reporter wearing a thick red snow jacket and a woolen hat. In the dark, she was standing outside, her figure illuminated by the bright camera lights. The snow blowing horizontally added to the atmospheric scene. She was shouting to be heard above the roar of the wind. "This is Ashley MacIntosh reporting from base camp. An avalanche has buried at least five tents. As you can tell, the visibility is down to a few feet. The fear is that the rescue team could be in danger if they attempt to search for anyone buried."

A gust of wind forced Ashley to lose her balance. She quickly recovered and grabbed her hat with her free hand to keep it from getting blown away. "The ice doctors, the Sherpas who prepare the Khumbu Icefall for the climbers, warned this could happen," she continued. "They said the huge seracs, the large blocks of ice along the path the ice doctors created, were unstable and could topple at any time. This was the likely source of the avalanche…"

The howl of the wind drowned out any further conversation

and the video image went back to the studio. "Thank you, Ashley," said the news anchor. "So far this year five people have died climbing Mount Everest, and five other climbers are missing. This brings the total number of fatalities to…"

A knock at the door interrupted Jerico's thoughts. He turned off the TV. When he opened the door, it surprised him to see Sergio Leone. That familiar sinking feeling resurfaced, just like it had during their previous encounter. Without saying a word, Sergio walked into the room and sat down in the chair in front of the fireplace. Jerico glared at him as he put his feet up on the coffee table.

"I did what you asked," said Jerico, still standing by the open door. "The news of the avalanche has reached CNN. Peter told me he watched it all happen from his telescope at the base camp. There's no way anyone could have survived. Did you see the size of the serac that came down?"

Sergio turned his head and his icy cold blue eyes glared back at Jerico. A chill ran through Jerico as he ran through the plausible reasons Sergio had come back. Jerico felt an intense pressure to explain himself and fill the void of silence created by Sergio's penetrating stare. He shut the door to the room so no one passing by could hear what he had to say. "I had one sherpa plant explosives at the base of the largest seracs. You know, the kind avalanche patrols used to stabilize the snowpack after a large snowfall at a ski resort."

Sergio continued to stare, making Jerico increasingly uncomfortable. *Doesn't he believe me? What the fuck is the matter with this guy? Does he need more details?*

"I had Peter keep me updated as to Eduardo's progress down the icefall," explained Jerico. "When they got in the perfect spot, I had Peter position the drone outside. I controlled it from here myself from my laptop. I even saw John wave to the drone as if it were coming to help him." Jerico let out a nervous cackle. "What an idiot!" Jerico's eyes flickered nervously, looking for a clue as to what Sergio wanted from him.

"When they got under the serac, I set off the explosion with the remote," he continued. "Want to see what it looked like?"

Jerico walked to the table next to where Sergio sat and flipped open the laptop. Sergio took his penetrating stare off Jerico and focused on the laptop screen. The drone video played.

"See, there's John waving to us, thinking he is in the clear."

The image of John became smaller as the drone gained elevation. The video focused on the 60-foot serac that towered over John, who was pulling the medivac sled along the snow pathway. As they passed the midway point of the serac, a small puff of black smoke drifted up at the base of the serac. A few seconds later, deep cracks appeared in the wall of ice. In slow motion, the face of the ice wall disintegrated, revealing massive chunks of ice hurtling towards the two men below. Within just half a minute, the drone videoed the powerful avalanche descending the icefall, creating a blinding cloud of snow and ice pellets that consumed the entire landscape and erased everything in its wake.

Jerico watched in stunned silence. The destruction was much more extensive than he appreciated from when he viewed it the first time. *Maybe I used too many explosives? I did what he asked and even took out John, which wasn't part of the deal. There are no witnesses now.* The video captured the mesmerizing sight of the snow and ice swirling into the atmosphere, completely engulfing the drone. In an instant, the white background turned black.

"The avalanche sucked the drone into the vacuum it created." Glancing up at Sergio to gauge his reaction, Jerico explained, "I think the drone must have crashed." Jerico paused for a moment. "You see? There is no way anyone could have survived that!" Jerico shut closed the laptop with a loud crack as if to confirm the point.

Sergio stood up suddenly beside Jerico. He picked up the laptop and threw it onto the floor. The computer shattered as bits of black plastic flew across the room. Sergio grabbed Jerico by his lapels and lifted the short man off the ground. Jerico quivered in fear as Sergio raged. "You told me we could trust Peter!" Spittle from Sergio's mouth sprayed over Jerico's face. "You said he would do as you asked!"

Jerico had difficulty breathing as Sergio tightened his grip on the lapels and lifted him higher off the ground. The tightness in his throat made it impossible for him to catch his breath. Jerico's legs kicked madly, knocking over the coffee table as he felt his consciousness slip away. A few seconds later, he felt himself go limp, and he slipped into the darkness.

When he woke up, he found himself crumpled in a heap on the floor. He reached up to his neck with both hands, gently massaging the sore muscles. He could feel welts on the skin of the neck where Sergio had throttled him. *There's going to be a bruise there*. Slowly, he sat up. He felt lightheaded, which passed after a minute. He stood up, trembling, and sat on the couch before he fell over. A wave of nausea flooded over him and before he could prevent it, he vomited his dinner, which landed on the white carpet in front of the sofa. He wretched several times before the nausea passed. Jerico slumped back onto the sofa. A layer of sweat covered his body and wiped his brows with his shirtsleeve before it dripped into his eyes.

"I too have contacts in base camp," said Sergio. "Peter left Everest ER less than half an hour ago to search for Eduardo and

John." Sergio was sitting in front of the fire with his feet up. He had fixed himself a drink of Scotch on the rocks while Jerico was lying on the floor. "I need you to clean up the loose ends."

Jerico shuddered as he knew what was coming next. He needed Peter to stay on as the Everest ER doctor. The $1 million he had invested in keeping the clinic was a cover to collect black heroin. If something happened to Peter, his investment would be in jeopardy. Jerico held dark secrets about Peter that he hadn't revealed to anyone, giving him control over the doctor's actions. By displaying the picture of his parents, Jerico's aim was to deceive Sergio into believing that Peter was willing to cooperate. Jerico was the only person who knew the genuine motive behind Peter's compliance.

The silence continued. Jerico was afraid to speak. He held onto the hope that Sergio would choose not to vocalize his thoughts; he was afraid of what the psychopath was going to say. Finally, Sergio got up and walked to the door.

"I expect you to kill Peter. Do not fail me this time." Sergio opened the door and left without closing it.

Chapter Fifteen

Eduardo looked down at his feet. His toes were incredibly itchy. It took all his resolve not to scratch them. The frozen skin that had been solid white was now replaced with a cherry red colour and was showing the beginnings of blisters.

"I need you to come over here," said Peter as he patted the gurney mattress.

Eduardo pulled his feet out of the water and dried them with a towel. He hobbled over to the gurney, and Peter helped him up. "I'm going to do two things," said Peter. "I'm going to dress your toes, and I'm going to set your arm fracture and put it in a cast. Which one do you want me to do first?"

Eduardo thought about it for a moment. "Let's do the feet first. I need to suppress the urge to scratch the intense itching. Maybe the dressing will help that."

Peter said, "Frostbite is very common up here. The itching will stop in a few hours and a dull ache will replace it. The positive part is that your toes will survive. A lot of climbers get gangrene and I've amputated more toes and fingers than I can count on two hands. I think you are lucky."

Eduardo squirmed uncomfortably at the thought of losing his toes. He knew with modern gear, most climbers could keep the toes and fingers from freezing. At high altitude, the problem frequently occurred because of low blood oxygen levels and insufficient oxygen supply to the tissues caused by a weak circulatory system. The strenuous effort from climbing caused sweat to accumulate, which could freeze later. The combination of poor circulation and dampness was a recipe for frozen toes and subsequent gangrene.

Peter applied Polysporin antibacterial ointment to all the affected toes. Next, he layered Vaseline-soaked gauze so the dressing wouldn't stick, then he wrapped the toes in a bulky bandage with cling dressing. Peter pulled socks over top so the dressing would stay in place and fastened boots over socks. "I'll lend you a pair of my boots until you get yours back. Now for the broken arm."

Eduardo looked over at John, who now lay on a gurney on the opposite side of the tent. Fluid from an IV flowed into his right arm. He had watched as Peter performed some neurological tests on John when they first arrived. As expected, Peter had diagnosed John with moderate high-altitude cerebral edema, or HACE, and administered a dose of dexamethasone intravenously. He gave John more Advil and Diamox pills, too. John appeared to be sleeping and seemed less restless. There was oxygen flowing with nasal prongs, attached to a bottle beside the bed. The oximeter read an O2 saturation of 95 per cent and a pulse rate of 80. Eduardo sighed. *Thankfully, he seems stable.*

Peter helped Eduardo shrug out of his coat. Then he removed his arm sling, untying the prayer flags that were lashed together to hold the aluminum pole splinting the fracture. He helped Eduardo remove his sweater and shirt. His arm had a slight bend where the radius had broken. "I think I will apply a plaster cast. It is difficult to tell the damage without an X-ray. Sometimes, to align the bones, we use propofol and set the fracture. But other times surgery is necessary to use plates and screws to keep it straight."

Peter poured warm water into a bowel. He wrapped Eduardo's arm with a soft cloth-like dressing. He soaked strips of dried plaster in the water and wrapped the arm with the thick, soggy white mixture until it covered the arm from above the elbow to below the wrist. "When that dries, it should immobilize your arm until we can get an X-ray." Peter washed his hands to get rid of the residual plaster.

"Thank you," said Eduardo.

"How's the pain?" asked Peter, drying his hands. "Do you need me to give you something?"

Eduardo just shook his head, not saying anything. He glanced over at John, who was sitting up on the side of the gurney, a crooked smile on his face. "Do you feel any better?" asked Eduardo.

"My headache is down to a dull irritation at the front. I still feel a little foggy," John said. "I think the combination of steroids and Advil is helping."

"We need to get you off the mountain and to lower altitudes as soon as the storm passes," said Peter. "The HACE will become worse over the next 24 hours. Eduardo needs to have the arm attended to at a hospital. I can arrange a helicopter when it is safe to land." Peter seemed a little on edge as he spoke. There was a slight tremor in his voice and he avoided looking directly at John and Eduardo. He was feeling unsure about where to position his hands as he continuously shifted his weight from one foot to the other.

"You seem on edge," said John. "What's the matter?" John and Eduardo were looking at Peter when he stopped shifting his weight and sat down on a wooden chair. He ran his hands through his hair and untied the ponytail. He placed his head in his hands and trembled. Sobs replaced the shaking. Their intensity was so strong that his entire body shook uncontrollably. Tears flowed freely down his cheeks, drenching his face. For the five minutes the sobs lasted, John and Eduardo observed without uttering a word.

Peter looked up at them with sadness in his eyes and said, "I am so ashamed." He hung his head and stared at the floor of the tent.

John and Eduardo shared a bewildered expression, their eyes meeting in mutual confusion. In a gesture of uncertainty, they both shrugged their shoulders, as if to ask whether the other understood what this was about. Not sure what to say, they remained silent.

After a few more moments, Peter looked up and said, "I've done some things I am not proud of, and now I am paying the price." As if unable to comprehend what he had just said, Peter shook his head in disbelief.

"Jerico's tight hold on me made me feel powerless, forcing me to go along with his wishes against my will," he continued.

Eduardo looked confused. "Who's Jerico?"

"Jerico owns 60 per cent of Everest ER," said Peter. "With his $1 million investment, it seemed like a good deal to keep the place running, even though there was no way the hospital would ever turn a profit. I found out later that he was using the clinic as a conduit for the black heroin trade. Every two weeks, Jerico comes here in his helicopter and picks up a duffle bag full of the stuff and takes it out of base camp with the rest of the medical waste."

John looked at Eduardo and said, "None other than Jerico abandoned me at base camp. In a desperate attempt to save you before the storm hit, I pleaded with the helicopter pilot to fly us up to Camp 1, only to be met with Jerico's resolute refusal."

"It gets worse," said Peter. "Jerico told me that 'someone' was going to have an accident on the mountain and that I was not to provide medical attention." He paused and looked Eduardo in the eyes. "That 'someone' was you, Eduardo."

Eduardo felt a shiver go through his body. *Who the hell is this Jerico person, and what does he have to do with me? Is there more than one person trying to kill him?* "That makes no sense," said Eduardo. "I've never met Jerico in my life."

"I think Jerico was getting direction from another man," said Peter. "After the conference two days ago, Jerico summoned me to his room. There was another man with him who said nothing. He was a little older. I got an uncomfortable feeling from him."

"What did he look like?" asked Eduardo.

"He was tall and thin, with grey hair and piercing blue eyes that seemed to penetrate your soul," said Peter.

"Ah ha," whispered Eduardo. "Now I understand. That would be Sergio Leone. He's one of the most sadistic animals on the face of the planet. He has a fondness for poisoning his victims. Now it all makes sense."

The conversation stopped as they glanced at each other. John interrupted the silence and spoke. "Eduardo, what the fuck is going on?"

Chapter Sixteen

As soon as the hotel phone rang, Suzie jolted out of her sleep and promptly picked it up. "Hi, honey!" Her heart skipped a beat at hearing the familiar voice. Suzie had drifted asleep, and her mind was a little foggy. She was lying fully clothed on the bed in her hotel room at the Hyatt in Kathmandu.

"John!" Suzie cried. "Are you… Are you okay? Where are you?"

"I'm fine. I am still at base camp. It's 2 a.m. After I found Eduardo, I brought him back to the base camp. I'm calling on Peter's satellite phone from Everest ER."

"I was so scared. There was an avalanche on the news that took out a few tents at base camp. I was terrified you got stuck in it."

There was a brief silence, as if John pondered how best to convey the events to Suzie, the weight of his words hanging in the air. "I got the tail end of the avalanche as I was pulling Eduardo on the sled but did not get hurt. We were able to get back to base camp safely. I'm fine now. Peter gave me some dexamethasone for mild HACE."

Suzie knew he was minimizing his symptoms deliberately so she wouldn't worry. "We need to get you off the mountain before it gets worse," said Suzie. "I tried to get a helicopter yesterday, but they were all grounded because of the storm that was coming."

"Jerico is up to something," said John. "He instructed Peter not to help us, but the good doctor broke ranks and went out in the storm to find us. He helped stabilize Eduardo's broken arm with a plaster cast and dressed his frozen toes."

"Jerico's demeanour and lack of empathy are powerful indicators that he could be a sociopath," said Suzie. "We need to remove him from our lives."

"You don't need to tell me that. He tried to kill Eduardo. There is definitely a loose wire upstairs with him. Who knows what happened to make him that way? It must have been something awful. We need to avoid him completely."

"Forget about that asshole. I need to come and get you."

"They expect the storm to be over by noon tomorrow," said John. "Peter is going to keep us in Everest ER overnight, and then he will try to organize a helicopter to get us to Kathmandu."

"As soon as the helicopters are cleared for takeoff, I'll be heading to the airport to fly to base camp," said Suzie. "I'll stay at the heliport until they'll take me up to you. Call me first thing in the morning. I'll have my cell phone with me. And let me look after the helicopter. We cannot trust anyone else to do it. John, please be careful!"

"One more thing," said John. "Talk to no one."

The phone call ended. Suzie sat in front of her computer. She logged on to the weather channel and looked up the forecast for base camp the coming day. They predicted the winds to reduce to 25 knots by noon. *I hope that is enough for the helicopters to safely touch down. Whether or not the clouds clear will determine the outcome.* They predicted the snowfall would stop within the next few hours.

She picked up her phone and dialled Marco. It was 2 a.m. in Kathmandu, so it would be 4 p.m. in Toronto. The phone continued to ring, filling the room with an incessant, unanswered melody. Suzie needed some advice from her brother, so she left a message on his voicemail, hoping he would call her back soon.

The next website she looked at was helicopter rentals in Kathmandu. The first one was Himalaya Holiday services. It surprised her to discover that the round trip from Kathmandu to Everest Base Camp cost $1,500 per person for a group of five, with the cost increasing for fewer passengers. When Suzie tried to book a helicopter for the morning, she received a message on the website stating that they would contact her once the business was open. Despite trying a different company, EBC Helitours, she encountered the same outcome. With a frustrated sigh, Suzie angrily snapped the laptop shut, the sound echoing. She stood up and walked around the room.

Who is Eduardo Rattazzi? What is the real story? A swirling array of questions filled her mind. *John said they were classmates in the school they attended in South Wales.* Returning to the laptop, Suzie eagerly typed in her search query on Google, ready to find answers. The sound of her fingers tapping against the keys echoed in the quiet room as she sat at the small wooden desk, typing in his name. She came across a documentary about Eduardo on YouTube.

As she watched it, she learned Eduardo was not only the eldest child but also the only son of Gianni Rattazzi, the influential industrialist who owned many car manufacturers, construction companies, newspapers, and various other businesses in Italy. "The annual revenues skyrocketed past $60 billion, demonstrating the organization's incredible financial growth. Eduardo was in line to inherit the fortune," said the commentator.

The video changed scenes to show a large university campus. "Eduardo studied religion and eastern philosophy at Princeton University in New Jersey. He achieved a PhD." A picture materialized, showing a tall, attractive man with wavy black hair, proudly wearing a graduation cap as he accepted his degree by shaking the dean's hand.

The scene changed to an older grey-bearded man wearing a

dark suit and tie. "I first met Eduardo in Rome when I was the Iranian Ambassador to the Vatican." The caption at the bottom of the screen read: Dr. Hossein Abdollahi. "He knocked at my door. Eduardo was 26 years old then. I instructed the doorman to tell him to come back tomorrow, because it was Sunday, the day I spent with my family. The doorman returned to say the young man gave him a message, 'God opens all doors.' I met with Eduardo immediately. He told me he had changed his name from Eduardo Rattazzi to Maghi, after converting to Shia Muslim. He asked if I could introduce him to Ayatollah Khomeini."

The next video captured Eduardo in a kneeling position, while Ayatollah Khomeini leaned in to kiss his forehead. "That was the first time Iran's holiest supreme leader kissed a foreigner," continued the former ambassador. The caption under Eduardo read, "His first visit to Iran."

A picture of the automobile factory in Turin, Italy, filled the screen. "The Rattazzi family imprisoned Eduardo, confining him to their massive estate north of Turin to pressure him to change his mind about his religious beliefs. They claimed he was insane and eventually hospitalized him. He was told he would be disinherited if he didn't convert back to Christianity," explained the commentator.

The video that followed focused on a picture of Kenya's sprawling capital, Nairobi. "The news company owned by his father reported the Melindi incident," said the commentator. "They arrested Eduardo and charged him with possession of 300 grams of heroin. The newspaper alleged that it was a setup to discredit Eduardo, to deem him unsuitable for running such a big company. The story goes that Eduardo had made friends with some Australians who, unbeknownst to him, were drug dealers. When they were about to shoot themselves up with heroin on the street, some children were watching. Eduardo told the Australians it was their right to engage in drug use, but they could not let it impact innocent children."

A decrepit room with torn drapes and worn-out furniture filled the screen. The mattress was devoid of bedding. A pile of dirty dishes filled the sink. Unwashed clothing lay scattered on the floor. "Eduardo brought the Australian men to his room. Just as the police raided them, he threw the 300 grams from the window. Eduardo's fingerprints were all over the bag. Although a court later acquitted Eduardo, 13 others remain imprisoned."

A soccer match filled the screen, featuring a video of the ball rebounding into a net. The goalkeeper, leaping from the ground, narrowly missed, deflecting it. "Juventus soccer club, owned by the Rattazzi family, became Eduardo's passion. He was involved in the day-to-day management for several years until his uncle fired him. Eduardo found out several days later by reading his father's newspaper that Umberto, his cousin, was to be the heir to the family fortune. Eduardo was devastated."

The documentary flipped to a picture of Umberto, along with his wife and two daughters, sitting in a convertible sports car. "Umberto died last year from cancer at 32. Gianni, the family patriarch, is dying and not expected to live for more than a few months. Eduardo is now the heir apparent to the family fortune."

The documentary went on to explore the various companies owned by the Rattazzi family and the potential impact of the patriarch's passing on these businesses. Suzie's pulse was racing. Although she'd had little sleep, she was wide awake after watching the documentary. Her thoughts confirmed her belief. *John and Eduardo are in grave danger. I need to get them off the mountain.*

A knock on the door jolted her out of her thoughts. She glanced at her watch. It was 4:30 a.m.

"Who is it?" asked Suzie cautiously behind the locked door.

"It's me!" said a familiar voice.

Suzie's eyes widened as she opened the door. "Marco!"

Chapter Seventeen

John woke up to find that it was already daylight. He glanced at his wristwatch. It was 7 a.m. His headache had gotten better, but he still felt a lingering dull pain in the front of his head. He remained connected to the IV, although the bag was now empty. Eduardo lay on a different gurney, snoring softly, with his boots laced to his feet and his arm in a sling resting on his chest. John quickly sat up, but the sudden dizziness made him immediately lie down flat. John made another attempt to sit up, this time taking it slower. Leaning against the wall of the tent, he swung his legs over the side of the cot, the fabric brushing against his back. Peter was not in the tent.

John peered out the window and observed the calmness of the wind, interrupted only by occasional gusts that whipped up occasional flurries of snow. The air was still and quiet, with no more snowflakes dancing through the sky. The low, grey clouds hung ominously overhead. Yesterday John had seen Lhotse, the mountain closest to Everest, while looking out the window. This morning, the clouds obstructed his view.

"Eduardo," said John. "Wake up."

There was no response from Eduardo. "Wake up!" John shouted.

John watched as Eduardo opened his eyes and sat up.

"Morning," he said, rubbing his eyes with his one good hand.

"How are you feeling?" asked John.

"Not bad, considering… I can't believe we are both alive," he responded.

"Where's Peter…?" asked John.

Eduardo barely had time to open his mouth before the door creaked open and Peter strolled inside. With a firm grip, he carried three plates, their warmth seeping through the edges of the tinfoil covers in wisps of steam. "Breakfast, hot off my stove." He put the plates on the little table and set up three chairs for them to sit on.

John rose cautiously, but felt unstable. Peter, upon seeing him wobble, came over and gently assisted him into the wooden chair. Eduardo hopped off the gurney and sat down beside the two of them. John lifted the tinfoil. The plate was a feast for the senses, piled high with fluffy scrambled eggs, golden toast, and fragrant roasted potatoes. The tantalizing scent of delicious food wafted through the air, making his stomach growl. He was famished, having not eaten in almost 24 hours. Wordlessly, he wolfed down the food, as did the others.

"I'll make some coffee," said Peter. "I only have instant, and it's black. Is that OK?"

Eduardo and John nodded in agreement. "And Peter, thanks

for the breakfast and for taking good care of us. My headache is not as bad as it was last night, so I think the dexamethasone helped, but the HACE is affecting my balance. I keep falling over," said John.

Peter looked away and shook his head. "Helping you two was the least I could do." He lit the one-burner stove and filled a small kettle with water. "John, let me give you another shot of Dexamethasone. It seems to have helped a little," said Peter. "But we still have to get you off the mountain before the HACE gets worse."

"What's the chance of getting out of here today?" asked John.

"The clouds are too low, so the helicopters cannot safely land," said Peter. "The weather report suggests that by noon it may have cleared up enough for a shot at getting a helicopter with any luck."

"Let me call Suzie," said John. "She'll be at the heliport by now."

Peter walked to the satellite phone stand and handed the device to John; he called Suzie's mobile phone. The phone was on speaker mode, allowing everyone else in the room to hear the ringing sound. Suzie answered. "Hi, honey," said John. "I'm here with Peter and Eduardo. We are all doing well. Where are you?"

"I just got to the heliport. The receptionist at Himalayan Holidays called me at 6 a.m., as she promised, and it won't be clear enough to take off until around 2 p.m. I asked if we could try for an earlier time on the off chance the weather improves. I offered to pay extra. She said we would have to wait and see. I put down a deposit of $3,000 to ensure I would have the first crack at getting a helicopter. John, I am so worried."

"That is the best and most reliable helicopter service," said Peter. "Count on them to offer sound advice that you can trust without hesitation. Let Marg, the receptionist, know you have spoken with me and that we have suffered several casualties because of the recent avalanche. To keep John and Eduardo out of the picture, you can tell her the injured were inside one of the five tents that were struck last night. Getting Eduardo and John to Kathmandu must be our top priority. Tell Marg to keep this information off the airwaves. If Jerico suspected that Eduardo and John might have survived, it would unleash a storm of trouble."

Silence filled the room. "Suzie," said John softly. "Are you OK?"

"I'm scared," said Suzie. The others could hear her crying into her cell phone.

"Honey," said John. "This will soon be over. If you can't get to us, neither can Jerico."

"Just be careful," said Suzie. Her voice became calmer. "I'll call when we get a time when we can take off."

John hung up the phone.

Eduardo spoke first. "We need to have a plan in case someone comes after us. The crew that left me on the mountain to die will be returning in a few hours. Hopefully, we will be long gone by then. There were four of them, including my climbing guide Angelo, who was in rehab with me. He was the one who convinced me to climb Everest. The two Sherpas… I had never seen them before, but one was called Pesang."

"Pesang!" blurted Peter. "He's the one involved with Jerico's black heroin transportation. He slept in the storage room last night. I'm going to see if he is still there."

"Hang on," said Eduardo. "He may not know we are still alive. If you disturb him, he might come after us. Let's think this through first."

Peter said, "We have pickaxes available to defend ourselves, along with flare guns and explosives. Pesang probably already left once the storm passed. I'll be back in a jiffy. I think we're safe."

As John got up from his seat, he struggled to maintain his balance and had to rely on the table for support. Through the window, he and Eduardo watched Peter enter the storage shed. A few minutes later, Peter returned to the Everest ER tent. He had five pickaxes and a satchel, which he emptied on the table, along with two small flare guns and a package of C-4 explosives.

"This might scare them off if anyone comes after us," said Peter. "The explosives have a remote detonator. The flare guns shoot out a fiery ball but will probably do minor damage except cause minor burns."

While they examined their arsenal, the door to Everest ER flew open, startling the men with the rush of sounds and movement from a gust of wind. As John turned around, his eyes met those of the man standing at the door, a curious expression on his face.

"Pesang!" Peter blurted. "I thought you'd left."

There was an odd look on his face, making it difficult for him to decipher his emotions. Pesang's eyes darted around the room, as if scanning for any signs of lurking danger. John and Eduardo stood in silence, their focus locked on him as the Sherpa closed the door and nonchalantly approached Peter. In a sudden motion, he swiftly retrieved a concealed knife from his shirt sleeve. As the light hit the blade, its sharpness became evident. It glimmered as he moved forward.

Upon seeing Pesang approaching, a gasp involuntarily escaped from Peter's lips. He slowly moved backwards until he reached the point where his body was pressed against the wall. "You don't have to do this!" Peter shouted. "There is a way out."

Pesang halted in his tracks, as if absorbing Peter's remarks. John and Eduardo watched in horror as Pesang, with no emotion on his face, swiftly lunged at Peter and plunged the knife into his abdomen, twisting it to maximize the internal harm. The anguished cries of John and Eduardo filled the room as Peter's body crumpled to the floor.

Chapter Eighteen

At the heliport, Suzie's persuasive words had convinced the pilot that it was a genuine emergency. Lives were at stake. The pilot's name, Andre Belanger, was written on the front of his black leather flight jacket. When Suzie had booked the flight with Marg, the Himalayan Holidays' clerk told her the pilot was from Belgium, but he spoke English, albeit with an American accent. She said he was their best, having served in the Belgium military for five years, a career he left to pursue a more financially rewarding job—flying tourists to Mount Everest Base Camp.

Andre had adorned the front of his helicopter with a painting of an open mouth, which showcased a set of menacing teeth. Suzie strapped herself into the front seat, and Marco sat in the back. The helicopter took off in a thick fog.

"I wouldn't normally fly in these conditions, but by the time we get to Lukla for refuelling, the weather prediction is that the clouds will have lifted," said Andre. His voice came through loud and clear in Suzie's headphones. "You understand that if it is not safe to land, we'll have to turn around and fly back to Kathmandu."

"I understand," said Suzie. "Thank you for doing this."

The helicopter flew over Kathmandu as it ascended over the foothills of the Himalayan Mountain range. The once breathtaking sight of the land vanished as the helicopter found itself surrounded by a thick blanket of grey clouds. The chopper bounced and swayed uncontrollably.

"Hang on!" Andre shouted into the headphones. "Once we are above the clouds, the turbulence should settle."

Suzie's body tensed up, her hands gripping the edge of her seat as a wave of nausea washed over her. She strained her eyes, attempting to fixate on the spot where the horizon should be, a technique she used to combat seasickness on the boat, but the horizon seemed to have vanished. Just as she thought she would vomit, the helicopter burst through the top of the clouds, revealing a breathtaking view of the mountains in the distance, their snow-capped peaks reaching towards the sky. As the helicopter ride smoothed out, her queasiness gradually faded away.

The higher they climbed, the more the tops of the hills emerged, painting a picture against the blue sky. Within 15 minutes, the scenery below them unfolded before their eyes, except for the valleys that were veiled in a sea of clouds.

"We are in luck," said Andre. "I can see Lukla. The airport is above the clouds. It is safe to land." He pointed to the 527-metre runway, flanked by modern buildings that housed various airport facilities. A twin-engine plane was taking off on the sloping runway. They'd built it on the side of the mountain and at the end was a

2,000-foot cliff dropping off into the valley. Suzie watched in awe as the airplane lifted off the tarmac just a few feet from the end. *So this is the reason it could be the most dangerous airport in the world.*

"Lukla is at 9,400 feet, so I would predict base camp at 17,598 feet will be free of clouds, too," said Andre. "We'll stop for 10 minutes to refuel, then we'll be on the way. You can both stay in the helicopter."

As the pilot circled the airport, a man wearing a reflective green vest and holding two aircraft parking wands guided him to the appropriate landing spot. The helicopter landed on the tarmac with a bump. Andre shut down the engine and the blades slowly stopped spinning. The cabin was quiet when Andre hopped out onto the ground.

They kept fuel for the helicopter in a large plastic drum. The attendant wheeled it to the side of the aircraft. Suzie watched as he manually pumped the fuel into the gas tank, the rhythmic sound echoing in the air. The process took about 10 minutes. Andre came back to the helicopter and pulled out a wad of papers from under his seat. He walked to the glassed-in office. From her vantage point by the window, Suzie saw him transfer the papers to another man, who then wrote something before passing them to Andre. Andre wrote something on the papers, then carried them back to the helicopter.

Andre hopped into the driver's seat. "There is a lot of red

tape when it comes to flying helicopters," he said. "We must prove that the service records are up to date before getting permission to take off after refuelling. Everything is about safety." He turned to Suzie and smiled. "Don't worry; we'll have you at base camp in less than 45 minutes."

As Andre started the engine, the deafening noise from the rotors drowned out any chance of conversation. Suzie and Marco put on their headsets. Andre spoke to the air traffic controller using the headphones and speaker on his helmet. He switched channels as soon as he was in the air and said to Suzie and Marco, "It should be a smooth flight."

The helicopter rounded a hill as it climbed up the valley. "There's Mount Everest!" shouted Suzie into the microphone. A thin layer of snow delicately flew from the summit of Mount Everest, creating a mesmerizing sight. Standing proudly next to Everest, the mountain of Lhotse loomed majestically. A fresh blanket of snow from the recent storm adorned the 8,500-metre mountain. The bright sun reflected off the brilliant white, creating a dazzling glare.

"There's Gorakshep, the last village before base camp," said Andre. "Many hikers spend two days here to acclimatize before climbing the last 3.5 kilometres to base camp. The trek is rocky and rough. With the low oxygen, many hikers become short of breath."

From the window, Andre pointed to a quaint assortment of stone huts, topped with roofs of emerald green tin, nestled 200 feet beneath the helicopter.

Suzie could see a group of 10 hikers making their way towards base camp, their backpacks bouncing with each cautious and deliberate step. Tied together with rope, a line of yaks trudged behind them, burdened with supplies. Two Sherpas, who used long sticks to guide them along the path, carefully directed the animals.

The helicopter continued its climb upwards, and Andre slipped on the nasal prongs for oxygen. "It's a requirement for all pilots to wear oxygen above 18,000 feet," he explained through his headphones. "Don't worry; you are in no danger."

As they flew higher, the Khumbu Icefalls stretched out before Suzie, a vast and awe-inspiring sight. Yellow and red tents dotted the bottom end of the icefalls, creating a striking contrast against the icy backdrop. In just a matter of minutes, she spotted the distinctive tent of Everest ER and immediately recognized the flat rock where they had landed during their previous visit. Andre landed the helicopter softly and when he turned the engine off, Suzie and Marco removed their headphones.

"I'll wait here," said Andre, removing his helmet and oxygen tubing. Reaching under the seat, he turned off the flow of oxygen and hung the nasal prongs on a hook above his head. Then he swung the door open, and Marco and Suzie bounded out onto the firm ground below. They made their way to Everest ER.

Chapter Nineteen

The sight of Peter crumpling to the ground, a knife embedded in his abdomen, had left John paralyzed with fear, unable to move. His pulse raced as adrenaline surged through his body. He struggled to maintain his balance, his legs wobbling beneath him. A wave of light-headedness washed over him. Pesang turned to face him, stepping over Peter's lifeless body. As he advanced towards John, another knife materialized from his sleeve and smoothly found its way into his hand.

John tried to move. A wave of dizziness flooded over him, causing him to lose his balance and collapse onto the ground. He lay on his back, gazing upwards, and watched as a sick smile spread across Pesang's face. John could see the knife in Pesang's hand, ready to deliver another fatal blow, this time to his abdomen. In a state of complete helplessness, he closed his eyes, seeking solace from the world around him.

Instead of feeling a knife piercing his stomach, it was Pesang's weight that slammed into John, leaving him winded and gasping for air as the knife fell to the floor with a loud clatter. He forcefully shoved Pesang to the side, causing the body to slide off of him. That's when John realized what had saved him: an ice axe driven into Pesang's skull. The blow was clearly fatal. Eduardo stood above John with a wild look in his eyes darting between John and Pesang's body. He was hyperventilating. The atmosphere was heavy with an eerie silence.

John was the first to move. He struggled to get to his feet, clutching onto the table for support. "Eduardo, are you OK?"

Eduardo looked at him and nodded.

"Help me check out Peter," said John as he held out his hand. Eduardo grasped John's arm with his one good hand and guided him over to Peter. John carefully lowered himself to his knees next to the doctor, who lay sprawled out on his back. John felt for a carotid pulse. It was present, but weak, his pulse rates an estimated 120. "Eduardo, can you get me that blood pressure cuff?"

John wrapped the cuff around Peter's right arm. The automatic blood pressure readout was 80/50 with a pulse rate of 126. The sight of the knife lodged in Peter's abdomen made John's stomach churn with a combination of fear and disbelief. Fresh blood oozed onto his clothing.

"He's still alive!" shouted John. "Let's get him onto the gurney in the other room. We can hook him up to the ventilator while we figure out what we can do to help him."

Eduardo rushed to the next room and returned with the gurney. John used it to pull himself upright to prevent himself from toppling over, while Eduardo lifted Peter onto the mattress.

Together, they wheeled him into the next room. A groan escaped from Peter as his eyes suddenly widened. It looked like he was trying to say something, but the words seemed to get caught in his throat.

John placed a tourniquet around his arm. "I'm going to start an intravenous," said John calmly. John inserted a 16-gauge intravenous catheter into a prominent vein in the right antecubital fossa. He swiftly connected a litre of saline solution and set the flow rate to its maximum speed. John went to the medicine cabinet and removed some drugs. He selected propofol and drew up 500 milligrams. He injected 100 milligrams into the intravenous. After 15 seconds, the effect of the drug kicked in. With Peter no longer moving, John used a laryngoscope. He slid a 7.5 endotracheal tube between the vocal cords and taped it in place. Then he hooked up the ventilator to the endotracheal tube and set the machine to deliver 40 per cent oxygen. John turned to Eduardo.

"I want you to record the vital signs every five minutes and read them out to me. If Peter starts to move, inject that white medicine, propofol, until he's still again. I'm going to try to stop the bleeding."

John was feeling a little more steady. *The dexamethasone Peter gave me this morning is finally kicking in.* John approached a cabinet containing surgical tools. He chose sterilely wrapped items such as retractors, sutures, sponges, suction tools, and scalpels. After opening the package, he spread the contents out on a sterile surface placed on the table. He thought about other surgical instruments he might require.

"The pulse rate is 130, the blood pressure is 70/40, and the oxygen saturation is at 85 per cent," said Eduardo.

"Could you increase the oxygen mix to 60 per cent and give him another litre of saline solution," instructed John.

John used a pair of scissors to cut the fabric and removed the clothing from Peter. The knife was protruding from his abdomen, positioned slightly above the umbilicus. A steady flow of blood seeping from the area around the blade was dripping onto the bed. John prepared for the surgery by washing the abdomen with a chlorhexidine solution, creating a sterile environment before placing the surgical drapes.

John could not find a surgical gown, so he removed his shirt and washed his hands and arms with chlorhexidine. He wore two pairs of size 8 surgical gloves, protecting his hands and extending halfway up his lower arms. He positioned himself on the right side of the bed and prepared himself to make the incision.

"The vital signs are getting worse!" bellowed Eduardo. "The pulse is 140, the blood pressure is 60/30, and the oxygen saturation is at 80 per cent."

"Increase the oxygen flow to 100 per cent and pump in another litre of saline solution," said John. "I'm going to make the incision and see what I can do."

John firmly gripped the scalpel, its cold metal glinting under the bright surgical lights, and carefully sliced through the skin, creating an incision that stretched from the upper abdomen to the lower abdomen. He hesitated to remove the knife, fearing that it would exacerbate the bleeding until the abdomen was fully exposed. Upon entering the abdomen, a gush of blood poured out. To control the bleeding, he reached up and carefully palpated the area where the esophagus entered the abdomen through the diaphragm, searching for the pulsating aorta. His fingers bluntly dissected on either side of the aorta. Reaching up with a large clamp in his right hand while his left hand retracted the stomach and liver to expose the area, he placed it on the aorta and squeezed it closed. Once he applied the clamp, the pulsation of the aorta below it came to a halt.

Eduardo's voice carried a hint of relief as he shared the vital signs: "The pulse is at 110, blood pressure is 90/60, and the oxygen saturation is at a perfect 100 per cent."

John had barely opened his mouth to speak when the thunderous noise of an approaching helicopter filled the tent. John looked up at Eduardo who simply shook his head and said, "Keep focused on Peter."

John used a combination of sponges and suction to mop up the blood in the abdomen. He removed the knife and placed it on the surgical table beside the instruments. The knife had gone through a loop of small intestine. John mobilized the small intestine to expose the abdominal aorta. The sight of the large hole in the inferior vena cava made his heart sink as he realized the severity of the injury. A significant amount of bleeding could be attributed to a large laceration in the aorta, which was near the hole in the vena cava.

It was then he heard a blood-curdling scream from the other room. *Suzie!* The sound reverberated through the room. John knew it was the shock of seeing a lifeless body in the middle of the floor. Its presence was made even more chilling by the pool of blood that surrounded it, and the ice axe impaled the back of the skull.

"Suzie!" shouted John. "We're over here in the next room!" Through the open door, he could see the look of pure horror on Suzie's face as she stared at the gruesome slaughter. His voice filled with urgency, he pleaded, "I need your help!"

Marco was the first to arrive beside John. "How can I help?" he asked.

John's surprise was evident by Marco's own reaction, but he quickly regained his composure. *How did Marco end up here?*

"I spent five years in the jungle as a leader in the revolutionary army and have field medical training," Marco explained to Eduardo. "Seen lots of knife and gun injuries from the confrontation with the government army. The mobile hospital tents were just like this. Of course, there were more doctors and nurses available, but I would frequently help during the surgeries when they needed me."

"Put on a pair of gloves then and give me a hand here," said John. "I have to sew up some holes in the major vessels. I need you to retract so I can get a good view of the injuries."

Marco washed his hands and put on two pairs of size 8½ gloves. He pulled them up to almost his elbows and walked over to the operating table and stood on the opposite side of the bed, facing John. He plunged his hands into the open abdomen and retracted the small intestine to expose the inferior vena cava and aorta. His right hand pushed on the sponges holding the bowel in place, while his left hand held the suction to keep the operative field free of blood.

John's eyes shifted upward, locking onto Marco's gaze, giving him a look of pure astonishment. "You've done this kind of thing before."

Marco grunted as if to say, "Get on with it."

At that moment, Andre entered the Everest ER tent. "Holy shit!" he cried out. "What the fuck happened?" He stared at the prone body of Pesang on the floor. Andre's eyes widened as he saw what John was doing. He quickly shifted his gaze towards Eduardo, his eyes flashing with intensity.

Eduardo said, "We are in the middle of emergency surgery. You must be the pilot. We'll need you to fly us out of here as soon as we finish. In the meantime, you can help by opening more surgical sponges for John."

Suzie stood at the door in a shocked silence. She glanced at John, who had both arms up to his elbows inside Peter's abdomen. In a display of genuine affection, John directed his gaze towards Suzie, his eyes radiating with kindness. "Hi, Suzie. Could you give Eduardo a hand if he needs more propofol or IV solutions? Could you empty the suction bottle and pour the contents down the sink?"

John went back to his task of repairing the vessels. Marco held the suction canula, keeping the operative field free of blood while John sutured the hole in the inferior vena cava. John used a prolene stitch and within 10 minutes, closed the hole in the inferior vena. John next turned his attention to the aorta. The laceration encompassed 75 per cent of the vessel. Starting at the back of the vessel, John used a baseball-type of stitch, closing the laceration with two sutures, which he tied in the middle of the aorta. The repair looked perfect.

"I'm going to release the clamp on the aorta," he said. "Eduardo, could you give another litre of saline solution before I do this?"

After Eduardo had given the saline solution, John slowly released the clamp. Looking directly at the repairs of the major vessels, they seemed secure. However, the abdomen quickly filled with blood again. Using sponges to absorb it, John pinpointed the source to a major vessel in the small bowel mesentery. He clamped it and inspected the damage. The knife had divided the vessel in two. It was large enough that John felt he should repair it rather than tie it off. Using the smallest prolene suture that was available, he sutured the two ends back together, which stopped the bleeding. A good pulse beyond the repair confirmed the repair was a success.

The last step was to reattach the damaged small intestine. John used an absorbable suture to do this. The severed small intestine repair looked perfect. John washed the abdomen with a saline solution before closing the abdominal incisions. The applied dressings covered the wound. He walked over to the sink, removed his gloves and washed the blood off his hands. He dried his hands with a paper towel.

"How are the vitals?" asked John.

Eduardo said, "Pulse rate is 100, the blood pressure is 100/60, and the oxygen saturation is 100 per cent."

John sat on a chair next to Suzie. "Are you OK?" he asked her.

"This is a little shocking!" she said. "I have never seen you operate before. Do you think Peter will be OK?"

"Don't know," answered John. "Most patients with this type of injury in Toronto usually die at the scene. Often, they never survive the ride in the ambulance to the hospital. By operating swiftly within minutes of the injury, we significantly increased his chances of survival."

Andre had remained quiet until this point. Confusion clouded his face as his eyes scanned the room, searching for any clues that could provide answers. "That's Pesang," he whispered. "I've known him for years. I know his wife and kids.

"He's the one who stabbed Peter," John explained. "He came after me with another knife, but Eduardo stopped him with the ice axe."

Andre shook his head as if he couldn't believe what he had heard.

"We need to get out of here," said John. "Peter is going to die if we cannot get him to a hospital. Can you fly us to B&B Hospital in Kathmandu? They have a helipad on the roof. I know the owner, Dr. Pansour. I'll tell him to expect us before we leave Everest ER."

Andre remained quiet, looking around as if trying to collect his thoughts. "We need to call the police," he said.

"I agree," said John. "We can call them when we are airborne. A man's life is at stake if we delay."

Andre agreed to prepare the helicopter. To accommodate Peter, Andre removed some bulkheads separating the cargo space from the back seat. Marco, Eduardo, and Andre worked together to carry Peter to the waiting helicopter, while John provided manual ventilation using an Ambu bag. Suzie sat in the front. Marco, Eduardo, and John sat in the back of the helicopter to take turns providing manual ventilation. Andre fired up the helicopter.

Within minutes, they were on their way to Kathmandu.

Chapter Twenty

"There has been a homicide at Mount Everest Base Camp," said the CNN announcer. "Three to five people die every year at base camp, usually from altitude sickness, but this is the first reported murder. Because of an ongoing investigation by the armed police force in Nepal, specific details are currently unavailable."

Jerico smiled as he watched the newscast from his suite at the Hyatt. He knew he could count on Pesang to take care of Peter. For the last two years, Pesang had been on Jerico's payroll. He had two kids enrolled in a private school in Kathmandu, and the money he earned as a mountaineering guide only covered a small portion of his annual school expenses. He depended on earnings from working for Jerico to pay the remainder. Every two weeks during the climbing season, Penang would transport the black heroin to the Everest ER storage room. By paying Pesang an additional $10,000, in exchange for eliminating Peter, Jerico ensured the guide's financial security for more than a year.

The CNN camera focused on the blond reporter standing in front of Everest ER. "This is Ashley MacIntosh reporting from Mount Everest Base Camp. Everest ER has turned into a crime scene." The camera captured a shot of the yellow police tape that was wrapped around the tent. A pair of law enforcement officers wearing protective blue hazmat suits carried a stretcher. An orange blanket concealed the body. The camera captured them as they marched by.

"The police have not released the identity of the victim until they notify the family and perform an autopsy," Ashley continued. "A reliable source has told us the victim suffered a blow to the head from an ice axe similar to the one I'm holding here." She proudly raised the tool axe she held in her left hand, making sure everyone could see it through the camera. "More details will follow when we have more information to share."

Jerico turned off the TV. He opened his cell phone and sent a text to Sergio. "Mission completed. It's on CNN." *That should keep him off my back for a while.* Jerico couldn't help but feel a sense of pride at how far he'd come from his humble beginnings in China. The plan did not involve letting someone as unhinged as Sergio destroy everything. He had poured countless hours of sweat and labour into his investment, and the thought of losing it all was unbearable.

As a child, Jerico toiled in the rice fields, up to his knees in dirty water. He remembered the monotony all too well and there was no way he was going to spend his life in such dreadful conditions. Being the only child his parents were allowed under the one-child per family policy in China, he had no choice but to join them in their daily struggle to make ends meet during the harvest season. Instead of attending school, they coerced him into labouring in the fields, the weight of missed education heavy on his shoulders.

Even at the age of 11, Jerico could already envision a brighter future awaiting him. Some of his school friends excitedly shared photos of luxurious mansions and sleek sports cars from America. The thought of a different life, one free from the wretched existence he had been born into, consumed his every waking moment.

Every few days, he had to carry six 50-pound bags of rice to the local market three miles away. There, his father had built a booth with weight scales, and he would sell the rice for the equivalent of $1 per 100 pounds. Jerico was 15 years old when a man approached him in the market. He wore western-style clothes: blue jeans, a thick leather belt, and a brightly coloured shirt. The slender leather loafers Jerico had only seen in magazines.

"I'll have 10 pounds of rice," he said to the boy. Jerico, who had been staring at the well-dressed man, finally tore his gaze away and scooped the mound of rice onto the scale, effortlessly proceeding to package it into a bag. The man paid him in coins and Jerico put them in a cloth sack with the rest of money he'd made that day. The central government controlled the price of rice and charging more would land his parents in jail. Jerico sighed as the man turned to leave. It was hopeless for him to think of another life.

It was almost as if the man could read his thoughts because he unexpectedly turned around and uttered, "You know, what you make in an entire year, I could easily compensate you for just a single day's work."

Jerico was afraid to speak. "What's the matter?" the man asked. "Why continue to waste away here when you have the opportunity to live a life of leisure and enjoy every moment?"

"What…? What do you mean?" stammered Jerico.

"This is your lucky day," said the man. "I work for a firm in Hong Kong. You've heard of Hong Kong?" Jerico nodded. "We are looking for hard workers like you to join our company. Because of its status as a British colony, Hong Kong operates independently from the restrictive regulations imposed by mainland China. A lucrative job can earn you significant profits."

With cautious glances, Jerico surveyed the market, making sure that he was not being watched by anyone. Recognizing that his chances of leading a fulfilling life were slim, he understood he had to find a way to leave this place. This could potentially be his one and only opportunity. "Where do I sign up?" he asked.

Several months passed, and Jerico found himself strolling through the bustling streets of downtown Hong Kong in search of potential clients for his new employer. Jerico had secretly entered the Hong Kong harbour on a container ship. Inside the cold shipping container, he found himself surrounded by 10 others, all teenage girls ranging from 15 to 18 years old. In the dim light, Jerico could see their faces, displaying a mix of fear and uncertainty.

"They promised us we would make a lot of money. Now I'm not so sure I want to do this," said the young girl who had wrapped herself in a blanket next to him, "but they've already given me a western name: Jessica." They were sitting on the floor, the boat gently rocking up and down. Jerico felt nauseated. "I'm only 15; I wish I had never agreed to come," Jessica sobbed. There were tears running down her cheeks.

Jerico asked, "What do you think they want us to do when we get there?"

Jessica went quiet, pursing her lips and tugging the blanket around her shoulders. "My parents instilled in me the belief that hard work and honesty are the keys to achieving happiness and fulfilment. Along with that, they shared the harsh reality that life was tough and making a decent living required a strong work ethic and perseverance. Taking what appeared to be the simplest route, they cautioned me, would bring nothing but heartache. That's what I am afraid of—what they will ask us to do when we get there…"

The employer had tasked Jerico with seeking single men and inquiring if they desired companionship for the night. Once Jerico paid the $1,000 transportation fee to Hong Kong, the employer would compensate him with five per cent of the matchmaking profits. At this point, he was halfway done with making that payment. It was a tough way to earn a living but significantly better than slogging through rice fields with no chance of a better life.

Jerico found he had a knack for finding clients. Positioned near the entrance of the Peninsula Hotel, he would soak in the bustling atmosphere and catch glimpses of the glamorous guests. A quick glance was all it took for him to pinpoint the prospective clients. Once he did, they'd engage in a back-and-forth discussion to determine a mutually agreeable price. Though he'd begin negotiations at $1,000, Jerico would agree to a price as low as $200. His argument centred on the idea that sacrificing price would mean sacrificing quality. Jerico had a folder containing pictures of girls in suggestive poses and displayed them.

Things were going well for Jerico. He was saving about $200 per month. It was 9 p.m. on a Tuesday when he spotted an obvious client. Exiting out of the Peninsula was a sharply dressed westerner in an expensive suit, his polished shoes clicking on the pavement. Somewhere in his mid-thirties, he waddled slightly with the beginnings of a potbelly, but his confident stride revealed the arrogance of a successful man on a business trip.

"Hey," said Jerico in English as he sidled up to him. "You want some company for the night? I have some gracious ladies who are dying to meet you." Jerico noticed that the man had stopped, and from his facial expression, it was clear that he was genuinely interested. Jerico glanced to the left and then to the right to make sure there was no one watching. Then he whipped out his pictures. "Here's the best one." Jerico showed a photograph featuring an alluring Asian woman who was kneeling on a bed adorned with white satin sheets. She pushed her breasts forward provocatively, creating a suggestive pose. "Yours for the night for $1,000."

The man said nothing but only nodded.

"Follow me," said Jerico. Navigating through a dimly lit back alley next to the hotel, the man closely trailed Jerico until they reached a set of stairs that took them up to the third floor. As the door swung open, an elegantly adorned reception area came into view. The girl who was sitting behind the desk was wearing a name tag: Jessica. "I'll leave you here," said Jerico. "Jessica will show you to Rebecca."

Jerico turned to leave. Just as he descended the stairs, a sudden commotion arose as a group of police officers hurriedly made their way up the alley. They immediately spotted Jerico. "Halt!" they shouted in English. Instead of facing the danger, Jerico quickly pivoted and sprinted towards the dead end of the alley. A brick wall stood before him. He quickly scaled it while two officers chased him. Jerico leaped through an open window in the building, landing with a thud on the tiled kitchen floor, startling the family inside. They stared at him in silence as he quickly stood up and darted out the door, racing down a flight of stairs and onto the bustling street.

Jerico knew the police would continue to look for him. He had an escape plan. A fake American passport that had cost him $100. With the money he had saved, he purchased an airplane ticket to Los Angeles and flew later that night.

Looking back on his journey all those years ago, Jerico realized just how difficult it had been for him in those early days. He was determined not to let someone like Sergio, a low-class gangster, ruin all his years of effort and dedication. While lost in his thoughts, a sudden knock on the door jolted him back to reality. *Finally, room service bringing me a bottle of champagne to celebrate.*

He opened the door, but to his horror, it wasn't room service.

"You fucked up!" Sergio shouted. Moving as fast as lightning, he coiled his right arm and unleashed a forceful punch onto Jerico's face, sending him crashing to the ground with blood streaming from his nose.

Chapter Twenty-One

John's headache resolved as soon as the helicopter landed on the hospital's roof. Although he felt fine, Suzie insisted he have an MRI scan, as recommended by the neurologist in the emergency room. To guarantee the complete resolution of the cerebral edema, the neurologist also advised admitting him for observation. However, John saw it as unnecessary since his balance and other symptoms of unsteadiness had already vanished.

The neurologist shook his head. "Although you feel fine, you still have neurological signs that suggest the presence of cerebral edema. The MRI shows the edema involves the corpus callosum and subcortical white matter. Look here." He pointed to an area in the middle of the brain. "There has been some micro hemorrhage extending beyond the edema. These findings may get worse before they get better. Some patients have had strokes from HACE."

John shrugged his shoulders. "I don't mind taking steroids and Advil for a few days, and if things get worse, I'll come back and see you. I feel fine… Really."

"OK. It's up to you. We are here if you need us." He left the room.

John glanced at Suzie and sighed, "Uh-oh…"

Suzie shot up from the chair, her sudden movement echoing

through the room. Anger flushed her face, turning it a deep shade of red. John thought he could see steam rising from her ears, a clear sign of her anger and irritation. "You almost died on the mountain because of your pig-headedness!" she shouted. "And now you are trying to kill yourself again. What's the matter with you? The cerebral edema has clouded your judgment. You are in no condition to make important decisions like that! I'm going to talk with the doctor." She moved towards the door.

"Suzie," said John calmly. "They are going to kill Peter and Eduardo. We need to stop them. While the threat is still lingering, I cannot simply sit around the hospital. I trust you more to look after me than I would trust the hospital staff, who are overwhelmed and rushed. The moment I feel I am not right; I promise I will tell you."

Suzie stopped and turned around. "I think you'd be safer in the hospital. Marco is here and can take care of anyone who comes close to Eduardo and Peter. Dealing with thugs and hitmen requires experience that you do not have. You even considered Jerico to be a decent and honourable man. You need me to protect you from yourself!"

"Exactly my point," said John. "I need you to keep an eye on me. I would trust no one else. I would not feel safe trapped in here."

Suzie sighed and sat down in the chair. She glared at John. He could see she was still seething, but knew she would let him have his way. "I was so worried when you jumped out of the helicopter to go after your friend," she said, shaking her head. She paused before she continued. "I am a little on edge from lack of sleep. Let's return to the Hyatt and rest. We can come back here later."

"We need to find alternative accommodations. Let's go to the Hilton and check in there," said John. Suzie nodded.

John and Suzie left the examination room in the emergency ward and headed towards the exit. "Code blue, ICU. Code blue, ICU," blared the loudspeaker.

John and Suzie looked at each other. "I hope that's not Peter," said John. "Let's check."

Suzie and John raced up the stairs to the third floor. A locked door restricted access to the ICU. John glanced around and saw an intercom. They buzzed to the ICU reception desk. "We are the family of Peter," said John. "We brought him down from the mountain by helicopter a few hours ago. We need to see him."

The door emitted a buzzing sound, unlocking as they entered the ICU. Peter lay in bed six, attached to a ventilator. The monitors showed a regular heart rate of 80. The nurse taking care of him looked up and said, "He seems stable now. We have given him heavy sedation, but the ICU doctor thinks we can extubate him in the next day or so. Don't mind the armed police guard. We often have this for our VIPs."

The Heir

A man in a blue police uniform caught John's attention. He stood a few feet away from the end of Peter's bed, with a no-nonsense expression on his face. Both his hands firmly gripped a heavy rifle. Taking a quick glance at John, he swiftly shifted his focus to the patient lying in bed number 11. John looked around the ICU. Every single one of the 12 beds had patients. In bed 11, the cardiac arrest team was actively engaged in performing CPR on a man on a ventilator. Even though the curtains were partially closed, John could clearly see that the code blue was for him, not Peter.

"That's great news. He is stable," said John as he glanced back at the nurse looking after Peter. "We heard the code blue and... Well, we thought the worst."

John walked over to the bedside. He checked the monitors. The blood pressure was 120/70, and the oxygen saturation was 100 per cent. Peter seemed peaceful with his eyes closed. John felt a twinge of anxiety course through his abdomen. Although he'd performed the surgery, he now had relinquished the postoperative management to the on-call surgeon, Dr. Prasath. Upon his arrival, they examined the post-operative CAT scan together and, apart from a few small areas of fluid accumulation, everything appeared to be normal. In response to a hemoglobin reading of 66, they administered two units of packed cells. John would have preferred to be the one in charge in case his condition deteriorated, but Dr. Prasath promised to give him updates.

Suzie took John's hand as if she could read his thoughts and said, "He will be fine now. Let's check on Eduardo before we go."

They took the stairs to the fourth floor, orthopedics. Eduardo was in a four-person room, but the other beds were unoccupied. Marco was sitting on a chair by Eduardo's bed. He stood up when they entered the room.

"John, how are you feeling?" asked Marco. "What did the doctor say?"

Suzie answered, "In his usual pigheaded fashion, John is not following the doctor's advice."

"That's not entirely true, honey," replied John. "He wanted to admit me for observation, and I agreed to the observation part. The only difference is that it's you who is the one watching me, not some distracted nurse."

Marco smiled and said, "Good to hear you are back to normal."

Eduardo sat up. His arm was in a sling. "Hey!" he said. "I'm fine, too! Don't you want to find out what they did to me?"

John laughed. "I spoke to the orthopedic surgeon after the surgery. He told me he had to position a metal plate to stabilize the fractured radius, but it should heal nicely. Suzie and I are heading back to the hotel."

"We're going to move to the Hilton," said Suzie. "It's not safe to stay at the Hyatt." *I'll ask the Hyatt to ship us our luggage and John's laptop when we know we're safe.*

Eduardo stood up and began putting on his clothes. "Whoa, whoa…" said Suzie. "No way. Not you, too. You stay here!"

Eduardo continued to get dressed. "I can't stay here, either," he said. "I, too, don't feel safe. Our best plan is to stay together until we are in a secure place. Additionally, I can offer the services of my personal bodyguard, Marco, to ensure everyone's protection." Eduardo chuckled. "I think we should all stay in the same room. What should we do about Peter's safety?"

"Dr. Pansour is part owner of the hospital," said John. "It was he who requested Mathew and I to perform the bariatric surgery for the course a few days ago. I told him about what happened to Peter when he met us on the helipad. I shared the entire story. Dr. Pansour assured me that the Armed Police Force would be constantly watching over Peter while he was in the hospital. I think he is safe for now."

Marco was looking at his cell phone. "I've booked a room at the Hilton through Expedia. Let's take a taxi." The others assisted him in gathering his belongings before they made a detour to the finance office to take care of the hospital bill. Eduardo handed over his Visa card to pay, and John watched through the open door as people walked by.

Suzie sat on a chair in the finance lobby office, engrossed in her cell phone. Vigilantly standing outside the office, Marco observed the people passing by with unwavering focus. He noticed a man looking around as he walked. His facial expression betrayed anxiety as his eyes flashed from one person to the other. He fidgeted with his hands as if he couldn't find a place to put them. The man brushed past Marco and stood at the elevator. Marco's phone pinged.. It was a text message from John.

"Jerico just walked past you."

"On it," was his response. When John looked up after reading the message, Marco was gone.

Chapter Twenty-Two

Suzie was fast asleep in one double bed, her peaceful breathing filling the room. John could hear Eduardo's faint snoring emanating from the other side of the room in the other bed. John had woken up an hour ago after just four hours of sleep. He sat at the desk on his computer, reading the results of his Google search on the Brothers of Italy party, or Fratelli d'Italia.

The ruling party in Italy had aligned themselves with conservative right-wing ideologies. They strongly opposed abortion and gay marriage, advocating for the traditional family structure. They regarded immigrants as lesser beings and advocated a zero-tolerance policy towards refugees arriving in their ports. Before Russia had invaded Ukraine, they were strong Putin supporters.

He googled Sergio Leone, but the only name that came up was the dead Italian filmmaker known for his spaghetti Westerns. Nothing about Sergio was on the Brothers of Italy website, or anywhere else. John read about his friend, Eduardo Rattazzi, which only confirmed the information Suzie had told him. When he researched terrorism in Italy, he found no mention of any political parties involved, only the typical warnings about mafia-related crimes.

"What are you up to?" asked Eduardo, rubbing his eyes.

Startled by the break in silence, John jumped up. "Eduardo, you caught me off guard. I thought you would still be asleep for a while longer. I was looking for information on Sergio Leone and came up with nothing."

"Not surprising," said Eduardo. "Many do not believe that snake actually exists. I suspect that is not his real name. He did some work for my father some years back when the union leader, Achille Grandi, threatened to close one of his automobile factories with a strike. On the night that a man named Guido Massone visited him, Achille Grandi tragically died in his sleep. The appointment of an interim leader led to the resolution of the dispute, resulting in the astonishing outcome of no shutdown ever taking place. Achille's daughter firmly believes that Guido poisoned him. Guido vanished without a trace, leaving no sign of his whereabouts after Achille's death. She is absolutely sure that he now goes by the name of Sergio Leone."

John glanced at Eduardo with furrowed brows and a concerned look on his face. "Do you think your father is the one who told Sergio Leone to kill you?"

Getting out of bed, Eduardo moved over to the vacant chair next to John. "No, definitely not," he said. "Balancing his conflicting values between business and family, my father is a complex man. A few months ago, my mother reached out to me and told me he was dying. She told me that as the oldest sibling and the only son, he wanted to make things right for us as a family. She convinced me to visit him at our home in Turin. I was reluctant, given the grief he has caused me over the years, but I'm glad I went."

"What happened?" asked John.

"With genuine regret, he apologized for the abysmal way he had treated me. He explained it was only when faced with the certainty of death that he finally came to his senses. He looked at me with pleading eyes, asking me to take over the family business. I couldn't refuse. It is what I have always wanted, a chance to prove myself. I had just come out of rehab, which didn't seem to faze him when I explained all that to him."

"How did Sergio get involved?" asked John.

"According to my father, there were individuals who strongly objected to his choice of appointing me as the heir. He told me to expect reprisals. When I told him my plan to spend the next few months climbing the highest peaks in the world, he strongly supported that, saying it would build character and prepare me for the road ahead managing the businesses.

"Sergio goes with the highest bidder to make the most money. I heard whispers that the less scrupulous members of the Brothers of Italy had clandestinely hired him, hoping to make me disappear. They feared that my affiliation with Shia Muslim would lead me to sell out to Iran or another Middle Eastern country. This right-winged party is intensely nationalistic and wants to make Italy a stronger economic force and will crush anything that might be a threat. They see me as a threat."

"What should we do now?" asked John.

Eduardo gave it some thought before providing an answer. "Although I worry about Peter, he's just a loose end. It is me they want out of the picture, so I am hoping they will leave him alone."

"Jerico is up to no good," said John. "Him showing up at the hospital means trouble for Peter. I tried texting Marco, but I didn't get a response."

Suzie sat up in the bed and yawned. "Don't worry about Marco," she said. "His best work is when he is hiding in the shadows. He'll get back to us when it suits him."

"Eduardo, what do you plan to do?" asked John. "Is there somewhere on this planet where you can find safety?

Eduardo paused before speaking. "My family has a summer place near Cagliari in Sardinia. The staff have known me since I was a child. In the last decade, I frequently found myself there after my father exiled me from our family estate in Turin. The armed guards have a longstanding presence, and the estate employs all their children. We generously remunerate our employees; it's beyond my imagination to conceive of them succumbing to corruption. They have always treated me like family."

"No way!" John quickly glanced at Suzie with surprise. Suzie and I rented a sailboat their last year. You remember Antonio in our year at school? He has a 41-foot sailboat in the marina. We met up with him, his wife and two kids and sailed up the coast for a week." John pulled out his cell phone and flipped through the screen. "Let me show you some pictures."

Suzie sat on the edge of John's chair to see the photos he was showing to Eduardo. "Here we are when we arrived, feeling disoriented from jet lag…" A picture captured Antonio playfully urging John and Suzie to down shots of a mysterious dark liquid, their faces lit up with wide smiles.

"Here's a video of the beautiful coastline as we sailed north," said John. "We had a great time…"

Eduardo said, "Pause the video there. No, go back a bit. Yeah, right there on top of the cliff; that's our place." He pointed to the small cottage. "The main house is set back from the cliff, but this is where I usually stay. During the summer, I'd spend hours watching the boats go by."

"I can't believe we sailed right past the place where you live. You were probably staring at us while we went by."

Eduardo went quiet after a few moments. "I doubt I was there then. I was in Thailand, getting hooked on heroin. It's all a blur, but I eventually made it back to Switzerland and checked into Clinic Les Alpes for a six-month rehab. That's where I met my mountain buddy, or at least I thought he was." Eduardo shook his head. "He left me up there to die." Eduardo paused and then looked right at John. "If it wasn't for you, John, well…"

Chapter Twenty-Three

Marco's gaze followed the man identified by John as Jerico. He entered the hospital's elevator and selected his destination floor with a firm push of the button. As the doors were about to shut, Marco quickly entered and positioned himself behind Jerico. The elevator came to a halt on the third floor. The doors opened. Marco could hear the faint hum of conversation and the distant ringing of phones. Jerico appeared agitated, his eyes shifting anxiously as he scanned the bustling hallway. Jerico turned left towards the area marked ICU, so Marco turned to the right, towards the operating room. With his phone camera focused on Jerico behind him, he could see him pressing the intercom button at the ICU, waiting to gain entry.

The door opened and Jerico went inside. Marco's heart pounded. He swiftly spun around and sprinted towards the ICU door. By jamming his foot in the closing door, he forced it to spring open again. Marco slipped inside. The ICU buzzed with activity, as nurses dashed constantly from the nursing station to the patients' bedsides. From the corner of his eye, Marco caught sight of Peter, who was still hooked up to a ventilator. There was no sign of Jerico anywhere. Marco felt a shiver run down his spine as he noticed the police officer standing by Peter's bed, his gaze fixed on him. With a rifle cradled in his arms and a pistol securely holstered to his belt, he was armed and ready for any situation.

Marco made his way to the elderly woman on a ventilator in bed number seven, next to Peter. He leaned over and pretended to kiss her on the forehead, and he whispered in her ear. For anyone watching, he was a loved one, offering words of encouragement to get well. Marco sat in the empty chair beside the bed, his back to the police officer. He used his cell phone to look behind him and determined the officer had shifted his gaze across the room. Marco adjusted the phone angle. Jerico sat in a chair beside a patient in bed 12. He was looking directly at the police officer.

Marco felt a tingling sensation run down his spine. Something did not seem right. The police officer and Jerico stared at each other; it was as if they knew each other. Marco watched as Jerico glanced around the room before focusing his gaze on something. Marco adjusted his camera to see where he was looking. All the nurses were sitting at the station writing notes or banging on the keyboards of their computers. He turned the camera back toward Jerico, but the chair he'd been sitting on was now empty. He turned the camera to Peter's bed.

It was almost as if everything that happened next unfolded in slow motion. Jerico pulled a syringe from his top pocket and was almost at Peter's bedside. He pointed the needle up and gently squeezed the plunger, as if to squeeze out the remaining bubbles of air. Marco caught a glimpse of Jerico about to inject it into Peter's intravenous while the police officer watched intently. Springing from the chair in a seamless and graceful manner, Marco soared through the air, traversing over Peter's bed, until he forcefully collided with Jerico, causing both to descend to the floor with a thunderous impact. As Jerico's skull collided with the corner of an IV pole stand, a deafening crack echoed through the ICU.

Witnessing the gruesome scene, Marco's stomach churned as he observed a torrent of blood and fragments of brain tissue slowly ooze out from Jerico's open wound. Marco's sudden action caught the police officer off guard, leaving him momentarily stunned. Marco saw him raise his rifle, the metallic click echoing in the air, as he rolled away on the floor. A loud and thunderous shot reverberated through the room, shaking the walls.

Marco's body reacted instinctively, propelling him upwards as he sprang to his feet. With wide eyes, the police officer stared intently at Peter, his gaze unwavering. Where Peter's head had been was now an enormous hole in the mattress. Marco stopped momentarily. *He just blew off Peter's head. This cop is corrupt!* In a flash, Marco threw himself against the police officer, knocking the rifle out of his hands. With a powerful swing of his right arm, Marco struck the police officer in the face, rendering him unconscious.

Marco stood up, his eyes darted around the room, searching

for other threats. The nurses had thrown themselves behind the desk of the nurses' station. Marco could hear them whimpering with fear. There was no one else standing. In a slow and deliberate manner, he made his way towards the door, carefully opening it before stepping out and descending the stairs. As he reached the main floor and walked into the lobby, five security guards rushed by him and into the stairwell, heading up to the ICU.

Marco walked outside to the driveway at the hospital's entrance, flagged a taxi, and hopped into the back seat.

"Take me to the Hyatt." The taxi driver's response was a simple nod, accompanied by a mumble that he couldn't make out, but Marco wished to keep his true destination to himself. After being dropped off by the taxi, he would stroll over to the Hilton, where the rest of the group had gathered. On the back of the driver's seat was a small flat-screen TV. A CNN news flash interrupted the program.

"This is Ashley MacIntosh reporting from Everest Base Camp," said the blond newscaster. "Recent developments in the investigation of the brutally murdered Sherpa have revealed the fingerprints on the ice axe belong to this man." A picture of Eduardo appeared on the screen. "The police are searching for Eduardo Rattazzi for questioning."

Marco glanced at the driver, who was skillfully manoeuvring through the traffic, completely oblivious to the news playing on the

TV. Marco turned his gaze towards the screen again. "Eduardo is the son of Gianni Rattazzi, the Italian business magnate." A picture of Eduardo's father filled the screen. The image flipped back to the studio.

The announcer continued, "The Rattazzi family runs the major automobile industries in Italy, including…"

"Drop me off here!" Marco shouted to the startled taxi driver. Amid the blaring horns of the cars that were forced to stop behind him, the driver pulled over to the side of the road. Marco handed him a wad of bills, exited the taxi, and walked toward the Hilton. He needed some time to think about what they needed to do. *The police here are corrupt and we cannot trust them. I'll need to get Eduardo, John, and Suzie out of Nepal before we are all arrested and never heard from again.*

Marco could see the Hilton hotel towering above the city skyline as he walked towards the downtown. Money was the reason they were out to kill Eduardo. He knew this from his past life as a rebel commander. Ten years ago, when Marco decided to leave his native Colombia, he'd been in a complicated role serving as a lead negotiator for the peace accord between the FARC revolutionary army and the government. A significant number of rebels expressed their opposition towards the negotiations. Juan Gonsalves, who held the position of second in command, actively voiced his opposition.

The narrative always centred on ideological principles of equity, human rights, and fairness, but the real reason Marco knew was about money and individual prosperity.

His job in the FARC organization was as the chief financial officer responsible for maintaining revenues—at any cost. The FARC army's principal source of income came from the drug cartels. In exchange for allowing the cocaine production to continue in the rebel-controlled mountainous region of Colombia, the producers would pay a monthly fee. Marco would work with the drug cartels to organize the kidnappings of prominent government officials or their families and negotiate ransoms. The FARC's revenues topped $1 million monthly, and deals were almost exclusively cash. A peace accord dried up their revenue source.

It was during one particular night that Marco made rounds in the compound they used as a command post. He constantly remained vigilant, keeping an eye out for individuals who sought to obtain personal financial gain. He heard a faint murmur of hushed voices from the closed cantina, which was usually reserved for communal meals. Then from his vantage point, Marco caught a glimpse of Juan and a member of the drug cartel engaged in a discussion. Through a small crack in the tent, he could see Juan receiving a substantial amount of cash.

The next morning, Marco confronted Juan in his tent. "I saw

you take a wad of cash last night. It's my job to collect it and deposit it in the safe deposit box. What the hell are you up to?"

Juan stared at Marco. "All of us are doing this now. Your so-called peace negotiations are going to put an end to a great opportunity. You cannot stop us. I'm giving you one chance to join us."

Marco shook his head in disbelief. He pointed his finger at Juan and shouted, "After everything we have fought for, you turn into a capitalist pig like all our enemies. You should be ashamed of yourself. You disgust me."

Filled with anger and frustration, Marco stormed out of the tent. The extensive corruption within the FARC exceeded his wildest expectations. This revelation served as a stark reminder that greed and personal gain are inherent human weaknesses that transcend even the most idealistic individuals. After several attempts on his life by those opposed to the peace accord, Marco left Colombia and moved to Canada.

Marco reflected upon his experiences and how greed has the potential to corrupt even the most virtuous individuals, leading them to engage in morally questionable actions. Walking inside the Hilton, he headed straight towards the elevator. *Given Eduardo's substantial wealth, there is a significant risk of him being exploited for financial gain. We need to get him out of here. No one here can be trusted.*

Taking a moment to retrieve his cell phone, he scrolled through his messages until he located the one that John had sent earlier. They were in room 1021 on the 10th floor, with a view of the city skyline. He pressed the button, smiling at a cleaning woman standing in front of the elevator. Her hotel pass card was partially sticking out of her back pocket. Marco pretended to stumble and accidentally collided with her. He quickly apologized and slipped into the elevator. Upon reaching room 1021, he used the pass card to gain access to John's room.

Marco opened the door and burst inside, startling Eduardo who had been talking and now stood there with his mouth wide open. He quickly scanned the room, his dark eyes flashing, looking for signs of danger. Finding none, he focused on John. "Peter and Jerico are dead. We need to leave the country. Now!"

Chapter Twenty-Four

Suzie unlocked her cell phone and entered the phone number. It got answered on the second ring. "Hello," replied the voice in his distinctive Belgium-American accent. "Andre Belanger here."

"This is Suzie," she said. "We need to hire you again. Can you fly us to Darbhanga, India? There's an international airport there. We have booked flights to Europe for later tonight."

There was silence on the other end. "Andre, are you still there?" asked Suzie.

"I heard you," he said. "I'm thinking. I'll need to get clearance from the air traffic control and have my flight plan approved. It would take about half an hour to fly there. Can you come to the airport?"

"We need you to pick us up at the Hilton. There's a helipad on the roof. We spoke to the person in charge here and explained we wanted to go to Everest View Hotel for dinner and wondered if the helicopter could pick us up. For $1,000 he agreed, but we could tell no one it was him who gave permission."

"I've landed at the Hilton before. Usually it's free to pick up hotel guests. What's going on?"

Suzie hesitated before she responded, uncertain how much

to divulge to Andre. "The police officer—the guy who was supposed to protect Peter in the ICU—blew his head off. We don't trust anyone now except for you. We are worried that we are next on the list. Can you help us? We'll pay you $10,000."

"Hmm… $15,000 and you have a deal."

"You have a deal. When can you pick us up?" asked Suzie.

"I'll be there in 30 minutes. Don't keep me waiting." He hung up.

Suzie glanced around the room. Marco was resting on the bed. John and Eduardo sat in the two chairs next to the desk. They were all staring at her, waiting.

Eduardo broke the silence. "Do you think we can trust him?"

"Well," said Suzie, "he helped us when no one else would. It took a leap of faith on his part to fly up to base camp when the low-lying clouds made it difficult to take off. I think we can trust him. And he hiked up the price. I don't think he'll be able to resist the money."

"We don't have a lot of options at the moment," said John. "If we go to the airport, the police might be waiting for us. We don't know any other helicopter pilots. I think he is our best hope in getting out of here."

"Do you think we need a visa to be allowed into India?"

asked Suzie.

"I checked out the requirements when we landed in Delhi on our way to Kathmandu," said John. "As long as we are in transit and in the country for less than 12 hours, we don't need a visa."

"What do you think, Marco?" asked Suzie.

Marco sat up on the bed and scratched his chin. "I think we can trust him. If he tries to pull a fast one, I'll throw him out of the helicopter. When I flew helicopters in the jungles of Colombia, it was a lot trickier terrain to negotiate than flying one to India."

"Let's go then!" said Eduardo.

They quickly got together what few possessions they had and checked to be sure they had their passports. The four of them made their way to the helipad. On the top floor, Marco used the pass card he took from the cleaner to access the helipad. They climbed onto the rooftop.

They were 15 minutes early. Ten very long minutes later, they heard the helicopter in the distance and wordlessly watched as it glided in, landing on the helipad. The pilot took off his helmet and opened the door.

"My name is Giuseppe," he said. "Andre couldn't get clearance for India. I fly there regularly, so he asked me to step in. I can have you there in about 30 minutes. He wanted me to apologize."

Suzie looked at the pilot. He moved his eyes around and looked to the left, fixing on an imaginary object on the horizon. His hands were in constant motion, as if he couldn't find a comfortable position. His right leg bounced up and down in a nervous tic.

"We arranged for Andre to fly us," said Suzie. "There is no way we are going with you. Guys, let's return to the room. This is not what we organized."

Marco looked at John. "Suzie's right; this is not what we planned."

John looked at Eduardo with a confused expression and shrugged his shoulders. Suzie knew John would not challenge her after she'd made such a strong and definitive statement. Marco's defensive mode was evident as she observed his eyes swiftly shifting from the helicopter to the door leading to the hotel.

"Let's go," said Marco as he headed to the hotel's door. Suzie followed, with John and Eduardo close behind. The door opened abruptly, catching everyone off guard just moments before they reached it.

"Stop right there!" shouted a man wearing a balaclava. He was holding a pistol and aimed it at Suzie. "Get into the helicopter. Now!"

Everyone stopped in their tracks. Suzie, who'd almost caught up to her brother, froze.

"No way!" shouted Marco.

The man in the balaclava kept his gun pointed at Suzie but turned his attention to Marco. "You—get in the helicopter first, or I'll blow your sister's head off!"

Marco glanced at Suzie. She simply nodded her head. Marco slowly walked backwards to the helicopter, arms raised at shoulder height, and stepped up into the back seat.

"Now you two," said the man, pointing to John and Eduardo. They followed suit.

"You're next," said the man, pointing to Suzie. She followed the same process and climbed aboard, sitting beside John in the last vacant seat at the back.

The man with the balaclava kept the gun trained on Suzie while he hopped into the front seat of the helicopter, across from Giuseppe. "I am going to say this once. If any of you try anything, I'll blow her face off."

"Where are you taking us?" asked Marco.

In the tense silence, Suzie could hear nothing but the pounding of her own racing heart as she sat before the man, his gun fixed on her. The pilot revved the engine, its powerful roar filling the air as the helicopter took off. With the aircraft banking, Giuseppe set on a course up the valley towards Mount Everest.

They are going to dump our bodies high in the mountains where we'll never be found, thought Suzie. She glanced up at Marco, who met her gaze and gave a simple nod.

He's got a plan.

Chapter Twenty-Five

Marco locked his eyes on the man in the front seat. His finger tensed on the trigger, aiming the gun directly at Suzie's head. Every few minutes, the man would steal a quick glance out the front window, diverting his attention from Suzie for a second. The pattern seemed unwavering. Marco waited until they were high above the valley before he made his move. As his fingers gingerly released the seatbelt, his gaze remained locked on the gun's cold, metallic surface.

Once again, the gunman glanced through the front window. In that millisecond, Marco leaped forward. With his large powerful hands, he snapped the man's neck with a twist, severing the spinal cord at the second cervical vertebrae. As his neck forcefully rotated, his trigger finger involuntarily tightened, filling the helicopter with an ear-piercing blast. With a sudden tilt to the left, the helicopter swiftly descended towards the valley, the window bearing witness to the horrifying aftermath of the pilot's shattered skull, his blood and brain tissue staining the glass.

Marco saw Suzie's mouth agape in a scream, but the noise from the helicopter's engine and blades drowned out any sound. Everyone wore their earphones. With a sense of urgency, Marco wedged himself between the two front seats, his fingers instinctively wrapping around the smooth surface of the cyclic stick. Suddenly, he recalibrated the helicopter's death descent, and the horizon ahead of him regained its stability. With a swift motion of his left hand, Marco forcefully grabbed Giuseppe and hurled him onto the lifeless body on the passenger seat. Then he settled into the pilot's seat, feeling the weight of responsibility as he took hold of the controls and directed the helicopter using the foot pedals. As Marco banked the helicopter towards the closest snow-covered peak, the icy cold view of the glistening white slopes came into focus.

Marco adjusted his microphone on his headphones and spoke. "I need you to push the bodies out the door when I give the signal," he shouted. "We'll dump the bodies on the glacier. I'll hover over the spot. Then, John, you can open the door."

They approached the glacier at 100 feet above the surface. "John, open the door," Marco commanded.

As John reached over the bodies, he felt the pilot's arm was wedged tightly between the door and the seat. "Eduardo," he said, "I need you to reach between the arm and the door to open it," shouted John into his microphone. "I'll pull on the arm up to take off the pressure."

Eduardo leaned forward. Using his uninjured arm, he skillfully located the lever. As he yanked it upwards, the door burst open, making a loud thud as it slammed against the outside wall. In a surprising turn of events, the arm that John had a grip on suddenly propelled both him and the body it was attached to towards the door with a burst of momentum. Eduardo made a reflexive gesture and swiftly reached out to seize John's belt. Eduardo's hands clenched tightly, his grip growing stronger as he held on with every ounce of his strength as John flew past on his way out the door. Eduardo wedged himself between the seats to prevent himself from being swept away. With lightning speed and agility, Suzie extended her arm towards Eduardo, helping him haul John back inside the helicopter.

Marco observed how shockingly pale John's face was when he finally grasped the nearness of his own demise. In a state of distress, John positioned himself in the rear seat next to Suzie, where he continued hyperventilating uncontrollably. Suzie took his hand and gave him a reassuring glance. After the realization sank in that he was safe, John appeared to calm down and settle.

Suzie, John, and Eduardo quickly strategized on how to push the other person out the door, while Marco kept the helicopter steady. The three of them were able to successfully roll him out. He plummeted 100 feet to the glacier. The body bounced slightly, making a single movement before finally coming to rest on the unforgiving surface of the glacial terrain. The other body, which was 50 feet away, was sprawled on the ground, resembling a swimmer in the midst of performing the front crawl.

"I'll turn the helicopter around so the wind will push the door closed," shouted Marco. He switched directions using the foot petals. In an instant, the door was forcefully slammed shut by the powerful gust of wind, producing a loud bang. Heading towards Kathmandu, Marco steered the helicopter downwards along the valley.

"Suzie, I need you to sit in the passenger seat at the front and punch in the GPS location of Darbhanga, India," said Marco into the microphone.

Suzie wiggled her way forward. She used the chart plotter to locate the airport and then employed the "go to" function on the GPS by using the pointer. "Entered," she said.

Marco cast a brief glance at the chart plotter. He made a slight change to the direction, following the GPS's suggestion to go further south. "We arrive in 55 minutes," he said. "When we get a little closer, I'll radio the tower for landing clearance."

"Got it," Suzie said.

"Now I need you to calculate if we have enough fuel to make it," said Marco. "The helicopter papers should be under the seat."

Suzie rummaged around and pulled out a zip lock bag containing a wad of papers. "Got 'em. Let me read…" She paused as she deciphered the information. "From what I can gather, the fuel tank appears to have a capacity of 60 gallons. During flight at a speed of 140 knots, it burns around 28 gallons of fuel per hour. Currently, our tanks are filled halfway, indicating that we have around 30 gallons remaining. Based on my calculations, the estimated fuel consumption for the journey is 25.6 gallons, leaving us with a remaining 4.4 gallons upon arrival. We will have a generous nine-minute window available." Marco saw Suzie's eyes widened at the narrow time margin.

"That's cutting it slim," said Marco. "If there are headwinds or delays in getting clearance for landing, we might have problems. Is there a closer airport? Check the chart plotter."

"I think that is the closest one to us, unless we head back to Kathmandu."

"Going back to Kathmandu would be a death sentence for us," said Eduardo.

"I agree," said Suzie. "Let's take our chances and get to India."

Marco let out a deep sigh. In situations like this, he was in his element, thriving and making the most of every opportunity. Making crucial choices that determine life or death, despite having only partial information. *What if the tanks have 28 gallons of fuel instead of 30 gallons? The margin would be even tighter, making the situation more precarious. When the low fuel light comes on, I will decide whether I should make an emergency landing or try to make it to the airport.*

When they were 35 miles from the airport, Marco picked up the radio. "Air traffic control tower, this is helicopter Whiskey Tango Foxtrot Alfa Bravo Charlie 35 miles north of you requesting flight following."

"This is air traffic control," said the voice on the speaker. "We see you on radar. We'll have you land at the helipad to the south of the airport on gate 12."

"Gate 12," repeated Marco. "Standing by on 121.5."

Marco glanced at the fuel gauge. There was less than an eighth left. *It's going to be tight.* "Suzie, can you check on the chart plotter to see where gate 12 is located? That's where we land," he said calmly.

He glanced at Suzie as she looked at the chart plotter and zoomed in at the airport. "Here," she said, pointing to the helipad."

"We'll have to skirt around the airport and approach the helipad from the other side," said Marco. He altered the course to fly in from the south.

Just as they were 10 miles away from the airport, the low fuel light suddenly illuminated. Marco could sense the tension in the air as he looked around and saw that the others were seeing the same flashing light. The fuel gauge was just a little above the E mark. He calculated that less than three gallons of fuel remained in the tank. *That should take us 12 miles. We have nine miles left before the airport.*

One mile from the airport, the tank showed the fuel was below the E mark. "I think we are going to make it!" said Marco. "Talk about living on the—" The jarring sound of the engine sputtering abruptly cut him off, signalling the imminent freefall of the helicopter. From their 200 feet above the ground, they could see the city sprawled out before them. As the next 20 seconds passed by, they dropped 100 feet, the helicopter tilting at a 30-degree angle, causing their stomachs to churn. Suzie let out an involuntary scream.

With a sudden jolt, the engine roared to life, and the blades whirled back into motion. Marco maintained a 30-degree angle, reasoning that the fuel tank contained just enough fuel to flow into the engine at that specific position. Gate 12 appeared below them. They were 10 feet above it. Marco smoothly straightened the helicopter to land. The engine stopped. Everyone gasped as the helicopter dropped the final 10 feet, hitting the tarmac with a loud crash.

Marco glanced around the cabin. Everyone seemed startled, their eyes wide and hearts racing, but relieved to be unharmed. "Is everyone OK?"

John opened the passenger door from his rear seat, hung his head over the door's edge, and vomited.

Chapter Twenty-Six

The aroma of freshly brewed coffee and tea filled the small lounge at the airport. They were sitting around a compact table, sipping their coffee and enjoying the aroma. The airport staff had swiftly escorted them through customs and immigration after they produced their tickets and boarding passes for Rome on their phones. With no curiosity, they simply accepted the explanation that the pilot would arrive soon, without probing further about the helicopter.

When he thought about how close to death they had all come, John became rattled, and his body trembled uncontrollably. Marco and Suzie had relaxed postures and serene expressions indicating a sense of inner peace now they were safely drinking their tea. They were engaged in a quiet conversation in Spanish, punctuated by bursts of laughter. John shook his head, disbelief evident in his eyes. His peaceful life was a stark contrast to their past lived experiences, where the line between living and dying blurred on a daily basis. He took small, silent sips of his coffee, hoping that the warm liquid would calm his frayed nerves. His cell phone chirped. He pulled it out of his pocket. *Mathew.*

"Mathew," he breathed into the phone. "Are you all right?"

"Dr. Hegland!" said Mathew. "The police are all over the Hyatt looking for you. Where are you?"

"I'll put you on speaker," John said. "We managed to get out of Nepal. However, I can't disclose our location in case our conversation is monitored. Just know that I'm here with Suzie, Eduardo, and Marco—Suzie's brother."

"The shit really hit the fan here," said Mathew. "Jerico is dead and so is that mountain man we met, Peter. The police won't release the details of what happened to them. Apparently, they were supposed to provide 24-hour protection for him while he was in hospital. What happened to Peter, anyway? No one is telling me anything."

John sat in silence, pondering his words. "It's a long story. I'll have to fill you in when I see you later. My advice is for you to get out of Nepal and return to Canada. Unfortunately, because of Jerico being the sole person with knowledge of our intended destinations, we have no choice but to cancel our trip to China."

"I expected as much," Mathew said. "The police brought me to the precinct for questioning regarding your whereabouts, but fortunately, I couldn't provide them with much information. All I could recall to them was the moment I last saw you bravely jumping from the helicopter to assist your friend Eduardo at base camp."

"A lot of things have happened since then," sighed John. "I recommend checking if there are any available flights departing Nepal today. Once we safely return to Italy, I will make plans to come back as quickly as possible."

"OK," said Mathew. "Stay safe and we'll see you soon."

They hung up. John glanced around at the others. "What is our plan when we get to Rome?" he asked.

"That's up to you," said Eduardo. "But I'd like to have you as my guests at our summer place in Sardinia. You can feel safe there. We can recover from all the trauma we've been through. To ensure our safety, we have armed guards stationed around us, ready to protect us if our secret location is discovered. My father is there. Sadly, he is in the final stages of his illness and the doctors do not expect him to survive beyond a month. His pancreatic cancer has metastasized, spreading throughout his body."

Suzie glanced at Eduardo. "That is very generous of you, but wouldn't you rather spend your father's last few days alone with him?"

Eduardo looked at his coffee cup before answering. "Not really," he replied. "For the past 10 years, my father has refused to acknowledge my existence. I have felt nothing for him but a deep sense of rejection. It wasn't until he was on his deathbed that he finally attempted to reconcile our past differences. For me, that was too late. The emotional distance he imposed on me has left me with very few positive feelings towards him. Having you around during the visit to Sardinia would provide me with the emotional stability I need."

"We booked off three weeks for this trip," said Suzie. "We have the time, don't we, John?"

He nodded enthusiastically.

"What about you, Marco?" asked Eduardo.

Marco's gaze first landed on Suzie, then shifted to John, as if he was silently assessing both. "You have seen the trouble these two get into when I'm not around," he said. With a gesture, he extended his arm and pointed his finger at Suzie, and then looked directly at John and did the same. "To ensure their safety, I must constantly keep them in sight at all times."

John smiled. As the anxiety from a few moments ago faded away, he felt a sense of calm wash over him. Marco was right. John felt a sense of comfort and security, knowing he was there. The moment trouble came knocking, he exhibited a keen sense of intuition and promptly took appropriate action. *This experience originated from him surviving in the FARC revolutionary army and helping successfully negotiate the peace accord. Just like Suzie, one of his remarkable skills is the ability to analyze someone's true intentions by keenly studying their eyes and closely monitoring the motion of their body.* It dawned on John that his survival during the escape from Kathmandu was solely because of the presence and actions of Marco.

"I think we are in agreement then," said Suzie. "Let's escape to Sardinia for the next two weeks, where we can unwind and rejuvenate in the tranquil atmosphere, leaving this ordeal behind us."

Eduardo's phone rang. He answered it without looking at the caller ID. His eyes flicked to the left and then to the right. After two minutes of listening, he said, "I will arrive within the next 24 hours. I'll have three friends with me. He then hung up."

Eduardo looked up at John with sadness in his eyes. "My father just passed away."

Chapter Twenty-Seven

John had his arm wrapped tightly around Suzie, as they stood on the cliffs mesmerized by the vast expanse of the Mediterranean Sea stretching out 100 feet below them. Sailboats speckled the horizon, their white sails contrasting against the calm, azure seas. As they watched the sunset, a warm breeze gently caressed their skin, a soothing contrast to Nepal's bitter cold. The few clouds on the horizon drifted by, transforming the sky into a breathtaking palette of pink, red, and purple.

Suzie breathed a contented sigh. "Stepping into this paradise feels like a breath of fresh air after the nightmarish experience of travelling to Kathmandu," she whispered. "I wish we could stay in this peaceful place forever." As John leaned in and kissed her on the lips, she felt a tremor surge through her body and her heartbeat quickened. Running her palms up his spine, she could feel the gentle heat radiating from his back. He smiled at her.

"Remember the last time we were here?" he asked. "We had just moved in together in Toronto and the holiday marked a milestone in our relationship; it was our first adventure as a couple. I remember the excitement I felt having you all to myself for two weeks, exploring the ways to please you."

"I still remember how you pretty much ditched your friend, Antonio!" Suzie recalled.

"How could I forget! While Antonio and his family savoured their evening meals at the local restaurant, we indulged in our desires on the boat, unable to keep our hands off each other."

"He must have thought we were crazy, giving up on the exquisite Italian cuisine to satiate our insatiable sexual appetites." Suzie laughed.

While watching the sailboats, memories flooded back to when he and Suzie had sailed past this very place two years ago. John had explained to her he'd already planned the trip a year in advance, before they'd become a couple. He'd hoped that joining a flotilla in Sardinia—which was organized by Antonio, another former roommate from their school days in South Wales—would reignite his failing marriage. But when his marriage fell apart six months before the trip, he couldn't get his deposit reimbursed. Shortly after they moved in together, Suzie persuaded him it would be unwise to let the money go unused. *Besides, I needed to find out if she was right for me.* The nights of passion, followed by lazy days on the sailboat exploring the coast of Sardinia, confirmed for John that he'd made the right decision.

"That trip was one of the best holidays in my life," said Suzie. "I had never known loving a man like you could be so fulfilling. I was oblivious to everything else that was going on around us. My entire world centred on you. I think you were just as blind as I was on that trip."

John looked at her quizzically.

"I never told you this before, but sometimes when I walked past Antonio, he would touch my butt," she said. "Growing up as a woman in Colombia's aggressively masculine climate, I knew better than to believe his attempt to brush it off as an accident. When he did it again, I was already expecting it. As fast as a bullet, I spun around and firmly clutched his shirt collar." Suzie grabbed John by his and gently pulled him up to demonstrate. "I lifted him off the ground and crushed his testicles with my knee as he came crashing down. It was a stroke of luck that there were no witnesses present when he released a bone-chilling, blood-curdling scream." With a gentle touch, Suzie loosened her grip on John's collar, ensuring he remained unharmed.

John shook his head in shock and disbelief. Looking directly into her eyes, he said, "I had no idea. I am so sorry." Her dismissive gesture of waving the back of her right hand into the air as if it was all part of a normal day in her life made him laugh. "Do I have to be careful when I touch your butt, too?"

"On the contrary, you have to do it more often," she whispered and kissed him on the lips. Suzie gazed contemplatively at the water. "His wife never spoke more than two words to me during the entire trip. I don't think she liked the way he looked at me, either. Especially after I bruised his manhood…"

"We spent most of the time by ourselves on the trip, as I recall. I'm surprised you found the time to practise your Jackie Chan moves," he teased, as he effortlessly executed a series of impressive martial arts stunts. Suzie smiled and shook her head as she watched John's weak antics.

Silently, they watched as the sun descended below the horizon. Once the stars came out, they returned to the cliffside cottage. As they stepped into the living room, it surprised them to discover Marco and Eduardo seated on the sofa. They glanced up at Suzie and John as they walked in.

"We thought you two went to the state funeral for your father in Turin," said John.

"Sorry to interrupt your romantic evening," said Eduardo with a mischievous glint in his eyes.

Marco's eyes flashed around the room. "I was able to talk him out of it," he replied. "Instead of Eduardo, we sent a substitute who had a similar physique and build. This guy successfully concealed his identity by opting for a covert appearance, donning dark glasses and a bulletproof black fedora. He is a member of the security staff who's been well-trained. But to take extra precautions, we provided him with a Kevlar vest and made sure he was fully armed and ready to react in case of an attack."

Suzie and John exchanged puzzled glances. "We thought that was all behind us now," said Suzie. "What happened?"

"Sergio Leone is up to his old tricks," said Marco. "Florentina, Eduardo's head cook, caught sight of him rushing through the San Benedetto Market in Caligari when she went to pick up fresh fish for tonight's dinner. Despite him following her, she relied on her honed training skills to effortlessly blend into the bustling crowd, leaving him behind. She urgently reported the sighting to Eduardo's security forces stationed nearby. Their sudden appearance must have frightened him. We think he promptly took the overnight ferry to Civitavecchia. As it turns out, it seems everyone here loves Eduardo. Nothing happens on this island without it getting reported to his security team. His arrival by private boat went unnoticed, but had he flown, the airport staff at Alitalia would have informed us."

Eduardo glanced at his can of Diet Coke and took a sip. "The Brothers of Italy are in the minority when they say I need to be out of the family business. Across the northern regions, the majority of shareholders want me to stay on in the family tradition. More than 1.5 million of the 20 million workers in Italy are dependent upon my family's companies. We are the largest dynasty in Europe—and I intend to keep it that way. This is the moment I have been waiting for all my life."

John and Suzie sat down. "I had an inkling about your affluent background when we were at the school from the gossip, but I must admit that the sheer scale of your empire is truly astonishing," John said. "Considering the circumstances, it seems logical that you should have a higher level of protection than just Suzie and Marco. You won't be able to rely on me. I am useless when it comes to assessing violent threats as you witnessed on Mount Everest."

Eduardo laughed. "Thanks to the three of you, I narrowly escaped death on multiple occasions. Trust is a rare and precious thing, and I can confidently say that there is no one else on earth that I would trust more than you three. It seems like nothing for you to place yourselves in harm's way to protect me. If only my father had felt the same way about me, well—"

The sound of his phone ringing interrupted. Eduardo answered and listened. After two minutes he said, "Grazie per avermi fatto sapere."

Thanks for letting me know, John translated in his head.

Eduardo looked up at his three friends and shared the shocking news. "The stand-in we arranged for my father's funeral has been shot."

Chapter Twenty-Eight

"We need to get Eduardo away from here," said Marco after the security guards came to the cottage to take him to the main house. "Inevitably, they will eventually come after him at this location. I thoroughly inspected the premises, meticulously examining every corner. The property would be no challenge for Sergio to breach."

"There are over 50 security staff roaming the grounds, and over 1,000 cameras," said John. "How could we improve on that?"

A look of astonishment crossed Marco's face. "I went down to the beach last night around midnight," he said. "Sneaking past the security staff, I made my way undetected from there into the main house. There are too many spots to hide and avoid the cameras, especially at night. The security staff, mainly composed of local boys from the country, are fiercely loyal to the family, although their security training is lacking. It would be a breeze for someone like Sergio to slip by them without raising any suspicion. It's too dangerous for Eduardo to stay here."

Marco, Suzie and John sat in the cottage's kitchen drinking tea. An eerie ambiance filled the room as the dull light from the fixture cast haunting shadows on the wall. As the breeze blew in from the Mediterranean through the open windows, the faint sounds of waves breaking onto the beach filled the air. "What else can we do?" asked John.

Suzie looked down at her steaming cup of tea, then locked eyes with John. "Do you think Antonio would lend us his sailboat?" she asked. "As I recall, he keeps it at the marina in Cagliari."

"After what happened on the last visit, you would trust him?" he said.

"Absolutely not. The man is a pig. Throughout my entire life, I have encountered his type, so I know how to handle those types of men. I have serious doubts that he would make another attempt, considering the outcome of his previous actions. I think if we could set sail to the mainland with Eduardo and not tell anyone, that would be our safest option. We could blend in with the sea full of sailboats. Then we can sail to that resort town, Tropea, and disappear in the crowds of tourists."

Marco glanced up at the two with some confusion. John explained what had happened during their last trip to Sardinia. Marco burst out laughing. "That sounds like Suzie," he said between chuckles. "I'm going to track down Eduardo at the main house and talk to him about my concerns for his safety. I'll be back soon."

Silently, Marco slipped away into the night through the kitchen door, his figure blending seamlessly with the shadows as he ascended the hill towards the main house.

John glanced up at Suzie. "I think it is a bad idea. You are usually right in your judgments of people. I certainly wouldn't trust him after that. I never would have pegged him as the type of person to invade your space and physically try to abuse you." John shook his head in disbelief.

"He is harmless and behaves like 80 per cent of Latin men in the world. You have no idea what we women put up with. It is a cultural thing for these entitled morons, where women are treated like objects for the sole purpose of providing pleasure for them. He got it way worse from me and he knew I meant to harm him. If we ever encounter each other, I can guarantee you he won't come within 10 feet of me. I'm hoping you can call him and he'll let us take the boat without him on board."

"I don't know. Should we take our chances with something else? Can you think of another plan?"

"Call him, John. Really, it's OK."

"Let's talk with Marco first. He had nothing to say about your idea."

"That's because he gets seasick. Remember the time I invited him to come racing on your boat? He vomited from the moment we left the dock until we returned."

"I'd forgotten about that," John laughed. "When we

mentioned sailing, it must have triggered some unpleasant memories—that's probably why he bolted."

"I can't think of a better plan," she muttered, her brow furrowing with concentration. "The entire island knows he's here now. If we try to fly out, or take public transit like a ferry, they'll be onto us. If we slip away in the middle of the night, like on Antonio's boat, no one will know."

John thought about that, hoping a better idea would pop up. Nothing immediately came to mind. He yawned and said, "Honey, let's go to bed. It's late. Besides, we have the place to ourselves now. We can make as much noise as we want."

Suzie stood up and straddled John on the kitchen chair. She leaned over and kissed him, sliding her tongue into his mouth. "You read my mind," she whispered after disengaging from their embrace.

Just as Suzie got up and grabbed John's hand to lead him into their bedroom, a loud explosion shook the small cottage. Suzie felt the adrenaline surge through her body as she rushed to the door. In the distance, the main house was fully ablaze with flames reaching the sky and lighting up the grounds around the house. She looked over at John, who stared at the inferno from the doorway and seemed frozen in his spot. Gunshots rang out from behind the house. John glanced over at Suzie with a confused look in his eyes.

"We need to find Eduardo and Marco," she yelled as she

took off across the lawn towards the house. "Stay here!"

Suzy's pulse raced as she sprinted. From out of nowhere, someone tackled her. She fell to the ground and rolled in the grass from the momentum. When she became orientated, Suzie leapt to her feet and crouched into a defence stance, ready to pounce on the perpetrator.

"Suzie, it's me Marco. Don't go over there! Come back to the cottage. Let's go!"

Suzie ran the short distance to the cottage with Marco. Eduardo was already in the kitchen. "We were on our way back here when the explosion happened," he explained to Suzie. "We need to get out of here now! Grab your passports and your phones and follow me!"

Having already gathered the items, John followed Eduardo, with Suzie and Marco right behind. Hidden under the rug in the living room was a trapdoor, which led down some stairs to the basement. "Nobody knows about this," said Eduardo. "I used to play here as a kid, 30 years ago." A dull incandescent light led them to a stone wall in the basement. Eduardo pushed on one stone and the wall opened to a passageway. Once past the opening, the stone wall automatically closed. Eduardo placed a metal rod against the wall and locked it in place with two sliding metal braces.

"We are temporarily safe," said Eduardo. "This passageway

will lead us to the beach just north of the main pier. Marco told me about the safety breaches he discovered. I just didn't expect them to come after me so quickly." He shook his head. "I hoped we could leave in the morning, and then they attacked."

"Do you have a plan?" asked John.

Eduardo glanced up at Marco. "Marco told me about Suzie's suggestion of escaping on Antonio's boat. I don't have any better ideas than that. Have you come up with anything else?"

John thought for a minute before he spoke. "I remember where he keeps his boat at the marina. The name of the boat is called *Allegro*. Once we get closer to the marina, I can check to see if the boat is there. You guys can stay hidden. I will come back and get you. If I can successfully break into the boat, we'll be able to set sail and escape. Later, I'll take the time to explain everything to Antonio, hoping he'll understand. It's been two years since we last talked."

"Ok," said Eduardo, "Follow me. It isn't far from here."

They hustled through the passageway in a single file. The stone tunnel was just tall enough for them to walk, and wide enough for one person. A damp, musky odour emanated from the stone floor, but it was clear to Suzie that someone had kept it maintained as an escape route in an emergency. The wall supported an electric cord which illuminated the tiny light bulbs, allowing them to see. The passageway seemed to descend at a slight angle. After 15 minutes, they came to a wooden door. Eduardo was about to open it when Marco grabbed his arm and shook his head.

"We need to make sure no one is waiting for us on the other side," he whispered.

Eduardo looked at Marco. "How are we going to do that?" he asked. "The small wooden shack on the other side of this door is a storage shed for extra tools, fence posts, and some outdated equipment. The door is not visible."

"OK," said Marco. "Here's what we'll do. I want everyone to go back into the passageway about 50 feet. I'll open the door and check out the shed and make certain there's no one around. Then I'll come and get you." Suzie, John and Eduardo nodded in agreement.

Suzie watched as Marco opened the door and then closed it again. After a minute had passed, Marco opened the door and gestured for them all to come. "It's clear," he said. "Let's go."

The wooden shed blended in with the wall; handsaws and other tools concealed it. It was in total darkness. Marco used the light from his cell phone to find the exit. "I had a look outside and saw no one. It looks to me that the marina is about 200 metres to the right."

"I'll check out the marina and see if Antonio's boat is there," said John. "You three stay here and I'll be back shortly." He turned to walk away.

Suzie grabbed John's arm. "Wait a minute. I'm coming with you. It will be less suspicious if it looks like a couple returning to their boat after a night out on the town."

John nodded. He grabbed Suzie's hand, and they both headed out the door. The shed was on the side of the cliff. A dirt path led them to the small sandy beach about 15 feet below. On the edge of the beach, they climbed over a few large rocks, and they walked through an unlit parking lot to the marina entrance. They found the door locked. Beside it was a panel with buttons numbered 0 to 9.

"What do you think the combination would be?" John asked, his eyes narrowing in deep thought.

Instead of answering, Suzie reached around the back of her head and removed the hairpin that held her thick black curls in a bun. The hair fell to her shoulders. She pushed the pin into the lock until she felt some resistance. A loud click came from the lock, and the door cracked open. John and Suzie walked onto the dock and closed the door behind them.

"I think *Allegro* is on D dock," said John.

Suzie and John held hands as they walked along the dock to D17. The Mediterranean mooring style, with the stern facing them, secured *Allegro*. It was a Beneteau 47.8, almost 50 feet long. Red cushions lined the seating in the cockpit. The lights from the dock illuminated the bright red dodger and bimini. Darkness shrouded the rest of the boat. There was a wooden plank leading to the stern. John and Suzie got onboard.

"I think the key might be in the propane locker," whispered John. He opened the locker. "Bingo."

John turned to face the companionway door. He inserted the key and it clicked open. John flipped a switch, and as they walked down the companionway stairs, the dim light flickered to life, illuminating their path.

"Looks like there is no one here," said John. He placed the key on the captain's table. He turned around and headed towards the front cabin. It suddenly opened. Antonio stood there in his blue underwear, holding an orange flare gun in his right hand, ready to pull the trigger.

John froze in his place. "Don't shoot! It's me, John Hegland, your friend!"

Antonio's eyes softened as he spoke. "John," he said. "What the fuck are you doing here?"

Chapter Twenty-Nine

Antonio was on the phone when John and Suzie returned to *Allegro* with Eduardo and Marco. "Just getting the latest marine forecast recording," said Antonio excitedly. "They update it every hour. We may have to motor for the first few hours, but then the breeze should fill in from the south. It should be smooth sailing to Tropea. It will take us 46 hours." He placed the phone face down on the captain's table.

"Do you have enough food?" asked John.

Antonio opened the large freezer, revealing shelves filled with frozen chicken breasts, bread, vegetables, and hamburger meat, creating a colourful display. An assortment of fresh produce and dairy products, including milk, cheeses, broccoli, lettuce, and tomatoes, filled the fridge. "We have enough to last a week," said Antonio proudly.

Suzie said nothing as she watched Antonio showing the others the stocked supplies. Something didn't feel right. Antonio seemed too eager to please. He avoided eye contact with her and did not seem to acknowledge her presence. His right leg was moving up and down when he was standing still, as if in a nervous tic. Suzie turned her back to Antonio and saw his phone laying face down on the captain's table. She picked it up as Antonio talked to the others, keeping the phone close to her body so he couldn't see what she was doing. The phone was unlocked, as he had just put it down. She scrolled to the last call and pressed redial.

"Hello," said the male voice as she pressed the receiver to her ear so no one else could hear. "Hello… Antonio?"

Suzie hung up. *The last phone call was not to the marine weather service. He'd been speaking to someone else when they arrived on the boat.* Suzie was confused. It was her idea of escaping from the island using Antonio's boat, but something was not right. *Who was he talking to? It was 3 a.m.*

The boat was leaving the dock. Suzie could feel its movement as the engine revved. She walked into the cockpit. The boat smoothly glided out of the marina, propelled by the powerful engine. The red and green channel markers guided them into the Mediterranean Sea. As Antonio held the steering wheel, John pointed to something on the chart plotter and engaged in a conversation with Antonio about the route. Eduardo, who sat in the cockpit, looked up at them. Suzie glanced at the foredeck. Marco untied the fenders and placed them into the sail locker at the bow of the boat. Using the lifelines to steady herself, she carefully made her way up to Marco at the front of the boat, feeling the gentle sway of the waves beneath her feet.

"Something's not right," she said. Marco stopped what he was doing.

Marco's eyes narrowed as he focused on Suzie. "What do you mean?"

"Antonio's too nervous. When I redialled the last number on his phone, it was a man who answered, not the weather service recording like he'd told us."

Marco glanced at the stern. As they sailed further away from the shore, they could see the lights of Cagliari twinkling in the distance. Suzie could tell the boat was on autopilot since there was no one behind the wheel and it would adjust every few seconds to maintain a straight course. *The others must have gone into the main salon.*

"Let me check it out," said Marco as he made his way to the cockpit and descended into the companionway. Suzie watched as he disappeared into the boat.

She spotted a gaffing hook used to pull fish into the boat. It lay on the foredeck. It was about three feet long and had a four-inch hook on the end. Suzie grabbed it and made her way to the forward cabin. She opened the hatch, which allows air to circulate into the boat, and slid feet first inside, landing on the bed. The cabin's lights were off, but the open door leading to the main salon partially illuminated the room. A surge of panic washed over her.

Marco was lying motionless on the floor. Suzie's pulse raced and a gasp escaped from her. Antonio stool over top of Marco, hyperventilating. He had a heavy frying pan in his left hand. John and Eduardo lay face down, strapped together with zip ties. The sound of their muffled grunts filled the room as they strained against the tight grip cutting into their wrists.

Antonio looked like a wild animal, with his eyes darting around the cabin. He slowly backed away from Marco, one hand fumbling on the floor until he found the plastic bag filled with zip ties. Suzie watched as he bent over and tied up Marco's wrists and legs. Suzie crouched down and advanced towards Antonio, raising the gaff above her head and swinging it down towards the back of Antonio's skull. Just then, he turned around to look up at her as she drove the stick down. The hook embedded into his left eye. A loud, blood-curdling scream escaped from Antonio, as he clawed at the hook, blood and vitreous fluid pouring out of the wound. Antonio fell onto his back. After a few seconds, he stopped moving.

Suzie rushed to Marco, who moaned when she rolled him over. Grabbing a sharp knife from the cutlery drawer in a single fluid motion, Suzie sliced through her brother's zip ties. He sat up in a confused gesture as he rubbed his wrists.

Suzie freed John and Eduardo. They both removed the gags that were tied across their mouths and jumped to their feet. John grabbed Suzie and hugged her tightly. "Are you OK?" he shouted with concern in his eyes.

Suzie simply nodded. "Antonio did not fare so well," she whispered. Her gaze followed John's quick glance in Antonio's direction. His eyes widened in horror when he saw the extent of the damage she'd inflicted on Antonio's eye with the gaff. Antonio lay on the teak floor, blood pooling around his motionless body.

John sat down. "Oh my God," he said, shaking his head in disbelief. After a few seconds, he went over to Antonio and felt his carotid artery. "He's still alive, but his pulse is weak." Antonio remained unconscious. John inspected his friend's wound. The gaff had forcefully pierced through his left eye, leaving a gruesome sight as the spike emerged below the maxilla bone into the cheek. "We need to get him to the hospital."

"He caught me off guard," said Marco, rubbing the gash on the top of his head. He stood up and glanced at John kneeling beside Antonio. "Let's think this through before we do anything. He would have killed us if Suzie hadn't stopped him."

"I wasn't aiming for his face," explained Suzie. "I was trying to whack him on the head. He turned around at the last second. Bad timing on his part."

Eduardo was sitting on the bench in front of the dinette. His face filled with fear as his eyes darted around the room. He said nothing, but looked up at Suzie. She sat beside him and said, "You are OK. We will figure out what to do. Don't worry." With a tender touch, she reached out and held his hand, giving it a gentle squeeze. John and Marco sat across from them. He and Suzie began talking quickly in Spanish. As the exchange went back and forth, Marco nodded in understanding.

"Here's what we are going to do," said Marco. "Eduardo and I will head back to the shore in the inflatable dinghy. We are only about five miles out. John and Suzie, you will call a mayday to the coastguards and tell them Antonio attacked you. In defending yourselves, this unfortunate accident occurred. It is unclear how deeply the corruption has spread, but our primary objective must be to safeguard Eduardo from any further potential threats. We'll connect in a few days after Eduardo is safe."

Eduardo's defeated gaze fell upon his hands, which were tightly entwined and continuously fidgeting. "I know a safe place on the island we can hide until we can figure out how to get back to the mainland. How will we contact you?" he asked.

"Marco will find us," said Suzie. "Don't you worry about us. You will be safe with him."

Getting up from the table, they went to the stern of the boat. A refreshing breeze greeted them with the sound of water lapping against the hull. John released the 20-horsepower dinghy into the water, feeling the tug of the ropes as they held it in place. He attached the fuel line and started the engine. It sprang to life, making a gentle purring sound. Marco and Eduardo climbed in.

"Do you know how to drive this?" asked John.

Marco smiled and grunted. "I know how to drive anything. Don't worry about me."

From the cockpit, Suzie and John watched Marco and Eduardo disappear into the dark towards the flickering lights from shore, the engine roaring in the distance. The sound of the engine gradually grew fainter, blending in with the echo of the wind and the waves.

"Let's make the call," said John. Sitting in front of the captain's table, he grabbed the VHF radio. "Mayday, mayday, mayday," he said in a calm but urgent tone. "This is the sailing vessel *Allegro, Allegro, Allegro.* We have an injury on board and need urgent medical attention."

Silence. It lasted at least 15 seconds. John was about to repeat the mayday call when the radio squawked. "*Allegro,* this is the coastguard. Go to channel 12."

Suzie and John sat in the cockpit for the 10 minutes it took the coastguard to reach them. A paramedic team with them manoeuvred Antonio onto a wooden stretcher and strapped him in, then carried him to the coastguard vessel. One person steadied the gaff in an attempt to limit any further damage while two others carried the stretcher. The vessel's captain said to John and Suzie, "You two come with us. Giovanni and Carlos, my guardsmen, will bring the sailboat back to port."

As John and Suzie hopped onto the coastguard vessel, the two guardsmen skillfully took command of the sailboat's helm. Within 10 minutes, the high-speed coast guard cutter was at the dock. They tied the lines to the docking cleats in front of the coastguard station. Just as they got to the shore, a police car arrived to pick them up, its flashing lights reflecting off the water.

The police drove them to the precinct and ushered them into a small, windowless interview room. Two chairs sat in front of the desk and one behind. Suzy and John sat down as a man in plain clothes walked into the room, the sound of the door closing echoing through the silence. He pulled out the chair and sat behind the desk, never taking his gaze off the couple.

Suzie felt a chill run down her spine as she locked eyes with the man sitting directly across from them, his gaze piercing and dark. It was Sergio Leone.

Chapter Thirty

Driving an inflatable dinghy was a new experience for Marco. In Colombia, he spent most of his time in the jungle. The mere thought of floating on the water would send his head spinning, followed by a wave of queasiness. The only time Suzie had invited him on John's boat for an evening sailing race a few years ago, he felt utterly miserable, vomiting relentlessly from the moment they left the dock. He vowed never to allow himself to be on the water again, yet here he was driving an inflatable dinghy on the open ocean without a hint of nausea. *It could be the adrenaline pumping through my veins, or maybe it's just the fact that I am the one controlling the vessel.*

"When you get close to shore, turn left and we'll follow the coast for about 10 miles to a small cove," said Eduardo. "There's a house on the beach. We'll be safe there, you'll see."

Marco had some difficulty hearing Eduardo over the roar of the engine, so he slowed to an idle. "Why do you think it would be safe there?" asked Marco.

"The only access is by water, as there are no roads," said Eduardo. "Besides, I have a special relationship with the woman who lives in the house at the end of the cove."

Puzzled, Marco glanced over at Eduardo. He must have

misread the signals. He was convinced Eduardo was gay. "I need to know more. How can you be sure this woman won't cause you any harm?" he asked.

Eduardo sighed and looked towards the lights of Cagliari as if for answers. "Before I came back from the high school in South Wales, the same one that John attended, I realized I was homosexual. Upon my return, I naively had the confidence to openly discuss my preference for men with my parents, hoping for their understanding. Their approach was anything but understanding. Instead, they wanted to 'reprogram' my sexual desires," he said, gesturing in air quotes, "after the damaging influence of attending a permissive British school. They sent me to see the woman who owns the house on the beach."

Marco noticed Eduardo was getting more and more upset as he discussed the incident. Eduardo nervously played with his hands and avoided making eye contact with Marco, as if he were afraid of being judged harshly. He seemed defeated, his shoulders drooping. Marco had no interest in Eduardo's sex life but wanted to keep him out of harm's way, so he needed to know the security risks to the place on the beach. "Look," said Marco. "You don't have to discuss this. I just want to keep you safe until we can get you away from here."

Eduardo appeared to settle with Marco's reassuring words.

"It's OK," said Eduardo, now calmer. "I was 19, and she was 35. That was 20 years ago." He softened at the memory and lowered his voice. "Flavia is still a beautiful woman, with black hair that hangs to her waist, framing a face that is flawless. It is almost as if she floats across the room with her perfect body swaying to music that's playing in her head." Eduardo laughed and nodded at Marco. "For a heterosexual male, she would be the embodiment of dreams and fantasies, lingering in thoughts for years."

Marco stared at Eduardo. He knew exactly the type of woman he described. *Isabella.* His mind wandered back to his days as a young FARC revolutionary in the dense jungle. Isabella was the wife of a commander in the revolutionary army; he'd tragically died during a skirmish with the government army. She'd taken Marco under her wings as he climbed the ranks of the army until she was killed in an explosion that was meant for him while he was negotiating the peace accord with the government. The grief that was consuming him became so unbearable he felt compelled to escape to Canada, seeking safety and the opportunity for a better life.

Eduardo explained, "From the moment she laid eyes on me, Flavia immediately recognized the futility of trying to change me. Not only did she promise to take care of me, but she also suggested that we could pretend to be lovers just to make my parents happy. She mentioned they compensated her well, and if I was comfortable with the agreement, we might proceed? I agreed. Over the years, I have made it a point to visit her on multiple occasions, notifying my parents initially to keep up appearances but later just coming on my own. Not only does she genuinely care for me, but she has also consistently covered for me on multiple occasions. I trust her.

"Does she live by herself?"

"Surprisingly, yes. She must have had a terrible experience at some point, because she once told me I am the only man *she* trusts. I know we'll be safe there."

The engine roared to life as Marco sped up, manoeuvring the dinghy along the scenic coast. It took them around 30 minutes before they began their slow journey up the cove towards the beach house. The sound of waves crashing against the shore accompanied Marco as he drove the dinghy onto the sandy beach, displaying his newfound boating skills. Eduardo jumped out of the boat and, despite having only one functioning arm, assisted Marco in pulling the dinghy to a small shed. "We need to hide the boat," said Marco. "This shed looks as good a place as any."

Apart from a collection of beach chairs hanging on the wall, the shed was completely empty. Marco and Eduardo dragged the dinghy inside and shut the door. "Let's go up to the house," said Eduardo. "It is not the first time I've come here for an unexpected visit in the middle of the night."

They made their way up a stone pathway illuminated by a line of solar lights that marked the path. The porch light was on. The sound of their shoes on the wooden deck elicited a loud bark from inside the house.

"That's Angus, her dog," said Eduardo. "He knows me." Eduardo lifted a potted plant and retrieved a key hidden underneath. The door swung open and an enthusiastic Rottweiler jumped up on Eduardo, knocking him over. Angus showered him with affectionate, sloppy kisses on his face. Eduardo sat up, petting the large dog as he excitedly wiggled around him like a puppy. "This is my friend, Marco," Eduardo said to the dog. "Let him smell your hand, Marco."

The Rottweiler tentatively sniffed Marco's outstretched hand, giving it a lick as if to say, "Let's be friends."

"What's all the fuss?" asked a feminine voice.

Marco glanced up to see a woman wearing a white bathrobe. Her dark hair flowed onto the lapels. Seeing Eduardo sitting on the floor with Angus, her face, which had an angelic quality to it, broke into a smile.

"Flavia," he said, "This is my friend Marco."

Marco shook her hand. "Eduardo described you as a beautiful woman, but you have exceeded the limits of my imagination." With a tender gesture, Marco gently lifted her hand to his lips and planted a delicate kiss on it. In the dimly lit room, he couldn't help but notice the faint blush that spread across her beautiful face. As they locked eyes, a tangible silence settled between them, amplifying the intensity of the moment.

"Let me put on some coffee," said Eduardo, interrupting the quiet. They walked into the kitchen and sat at the table.

"Sorry about your father," said Flavia.

Eduardo turned on the espresso machine and ground the coffee beans as he spoke. "You know how I felt about him," he said. "Although he tried to reconcile with me at the end, my feelings for him never really changed."

"I heard you are the heir to the Rattazzi empire," said Flavia.

"Only if I stay alive." Eduardo went quiet as he packed the coffee grounds into the porta filter and started the machine. "Marco is doing his best to keep it that way, which is the reason we came here. I didn't mean to get you involved, but like always, when I'm in trouble, you're the one I turn to. I don't know where else to go."

"Tell me what has been going on," said Flavia. Eduardo handed her the espresso in a demi-tasse and turned to the coffee grinder to make another one for Marco.

Eduardo talked as he made the coffee and then sat at the table with Marco and Flavia. Recounting all the events that had taken place after his release from the Swiss rehab centre to the escape from the sailboat lasted for two hours. Flavia silently listened to the story. When it was over, she simply said, "You two must be exhausted. Go to bed. We can talk more when you get up in a few hours."

She led them to two separate bedrooms. Marco laid on the bed fully clothed and was asleep in less than 10 seconds.

—

"Marco, wake up!" Marco felt someone shaking his shoulders. He bolted upright. It was Eduardo. "John and Suzie have been arrested. They are in jail!"

Chapter Thirty-One

"You must be Sergio Leone," Suzie said confidently to the man sitting across from them.

Sergio's face contorted with surprise, revealing his futile attempt to deny. A mix of anxiety and disappointment washed over John as he recognized that this interview was going to be anything but routine, with his heart racing and hopes sinking simultaneously.

"We have never met, I am certain," Sergio said, failing to meet Suzie's stare. "My name is Sergeant Pesce. I do not know any Sergio Leone."

Suzie's intense gaze remained fixed on him, as John studied the interaction, noticing Sergio's attempt to steer the conversation by quickly glancing at the papers in front of him, his pupils constricting. It was so obvious that even John, who was usually oblivious, could tell Sergio was lying. In a swift motion, he stood up and forcefully struck the door with a loud bang.

"Luigi, I need you to come here," he shouted in Italian. The door opened and a man in a grey suit appeared. "Take the woman into the other examination room and conduct the interview." Luigi motioned to Suzie, pointing his index finger towards the adjacent room. Suzie stood up and followed Luigi, never wavering at glaring into Sergio's icy cold eyes.

John knew they wanted to check his and Suzie's stories to make sure they matched. He had full confidence she'd tell the truth, and their versions would be close if not identical. He would need to stick to the facts but also be extremely careful about what he told Sergio.

Sergio sat in front of John and started the recorder. After asking him to state his name and date of birth, he said, "Tell me what happened tonight on the sailboat."

John focused his attention on Sergio, locking eyes with a determined stare. Sergio returned an intense, icy stare that made John pause and carefully consider his words before speaking. The man's actions were that of a cold-blooded killer, showing no mercy or empathy. There was only one explanation for how John had ended up being interviewed here. *The police were paid off. The system is plagued by corruption. This is not going to end well for me and Suzie,* he thought, as a sense of foreboding settled over him. John looked around the empty room as if he might find some answers, but none came to him.

"You are Sergio Leone, a hitman for the Brothers of Italy," John blurted out. "You have tried to kill Eduardo Rattazzi to prevent him from taking over his father's empire. I am not telling you anything without a lawyer of my choosing." John folded his arms in front of his chest defiantly as he watched Sergio go red in the face and stop the recording.

"You little shit!" shouted Sergio. "You have no idea of the trouble you have caused!" In a fit of rage, he extended his arms across the table and forcefully slammed both of his hands against John's ears with a resounding thud. John let out a piercing scream as intense pain shot through his body and through his skull, triggering a ringing in his ears. He collapsed onto the floor with a loud crash. Sergio angrily approached John and forcefully kicked him in the gut. In agony, John grunted and retched uncontrollably. His empty stomach left him with nothing to bring up.

Two uniformed police officers marched into the room and picked up John under his arms. They dragged him into the cell with the other men, dumping him in the middle of the floor, where he remained curled up in the fetal position, unable to move. The pain in his abdomen was excruciating. As John lay there, he took a moment to assess the damage, his body still and his mind racing. He listened intently. The only sound he could hear was the constant ringing that drowned out all other noise. The ear pain had lessened, becoming a throbbing discomfort instead. He inhaled deeply. A sharp pain shot through his abdomen. He winced. Slowly uncurling his body, he regained a straightened position. His stomach pain wasn't as intense, but John still struggled to lift himself from the grimy floor. He settled onto the frigid metal bench beside a man whose snores filled the air.

The Heir

A nauseating odour of vomit, urine, and unwashed bodies filled his John's nostrils, making him feel queasy, the chill of the bench seeping into his bones. Four others who were slumbering surrounded him, leaned up against the wall. The man next to him had a thin stream of drool trickling down his right cheek. His left eye was swollen and discoloured. The loud snores emanating from the depths of his throat indicated his bent nose, likely broken, was obstructing his airways, creating a noxious wind tunnel that assaulted John's senses with the stench of stale garlic, alcohol, and onion.

Baffled, John tried to make sense of how everything had spiralled out of control in such a short period of time. The encounter with Sergio Leone, which had taken place only a few hours ago, played on a loop in his thoughts. Prior to this, Sergio was a stranger to John, and Suzie had never laid eyes on him before, either. Suspecting that she recognized him, John couldn't help but notice the intensity of his dark gaze, just as Eduardo had described to them. Before Sergio had even opened his mouth, Suzie had already gathered a lot of information about him, thanks to her extraordinary talent for interpreting body language and non-verbal cues.

The nausea was subsiding, but John found it hard to ignore the pungent odour emanating from the man next to him as he contemplated the various possible outcomes. If the level of corruption ran as deep in the police force as he suspected, there was a real possibility of being lost in the jail system for months or even years. Italy had a modern legal system complete with judges and lawyers, but the absence of access to them, never mind widespread corruption, could spell a grim fate. Clinging on to hope, he trusted Marco would never allow that to occur. John felt a desperate longing for Marco to be in a secure place, safely tucked away with Eduardo.

He found himself thinking about Suzie. He had learned many things about her during this journey. She'd bravely put herself at significant risk to rescue him from the mountain, showing no concern for her own safety. He'd heard stories of women who were fiercely loyal and devoted to their partners, but she was the first woman he had been with who actually showed those qualities. He had been aware of her remarkable talent for understanding human behaviour through body language for quite some time, but he was truly amazed when she identified Sergio and could paint a complete picture of him using only fragments of information she had gathered from others. The way she processed thoughts was remarkable. He also knew he would do anything to keep Suzie safe. He felt a deep sense of sadness because he had involuntarily involved her in this complicated situation. It was likely that she was lying in a jail cell, which was just as filthy as the one he currently sat in, with drug addicts and violent women. John hung his head low in despair as those terrible thoughts ran through his mind.

Suzie had saved him almost from certain death by impaling

Antonio with the gaff. She possessed an incredible amount of resolve and fearlessness. He shook his head, realizing he couldn't have done what she did. The thought that would have crossed his mind was that there must be some sort of misunderstanding. His proposed solution to resolve the issue was simply to have a frank conversation about it. Suzie possessed the remarkable ability to view situations in a binary manner, perceiving them as either black or white. She consistently demonstrated the willingness to take any necessary action to safeguard her cherished family members. He had much to learn from her.

John leaned his head against the wall and realized how exhausted he was. They had taken his watch, along with his belt and his shoelaces, when they dragged him into the cell, so he did not know the time. He closed his eyes and fell asleep in seconds.

Chapter Thirty-Two

"State your name and birthdate for the record," said Luigi in English. Suzie fixed her gaze upon him, remaining silent and refrained from uttering a single word.

Luigi shook his head and said, "Look, I just want to know what happened. The coastguards rescued a man with a gaff stuck where his left eye used to be. I think any police department in the world would have the same questions. You were there. Can you tell me what happened?"

Suzie's silence filled the room, hanging heavily in the air. Unfazed, she never broke eye contact and continued to fix her gaze upon him. His right leg shook in a nervous tic, a clear sign to her that the silence was unnerving him. His gaze shifted away from hers, and he glanced down at the papers spread out in front of him, as if hoping they held the solutions he needed. It was clear to Suzie that she was the sole individual aboard the boat who could provide a description of what had occurred. Marco was unconscious, while Antonio was securing him with zip ties. Antonio had tied John and Eduardo together and they'd both been faced away from her when she snuck onto the boat.

"Have it your way then," Luigi said as he walked out of the room.

Alone and lost in her thoughts, Suzie couldn't help but wonder how John was faring, trapped in the same room as the deranged psychopath, Sergio. She worried because John lacked the necessary expertise to handle individuals like him. Whenever conflicts arose, he preferred open and honest discussions, aiming to find common ground. One thing she loved about him was his calm and composed nature, in stark contrast to the fiery arguments she experienced while living in a Latin country. She needed to shield John from the harsh reality of dangerous criminals lurking in the shadows.

Marco knew exactly what they were up against from Suzie's first telephone conversation with him. As soon as her brother had arrived to help, Suzie felt reassured that her initial evaluation had not been an overreaction. Marco had pegged the Nepali police force as corrupt. He knew what to do in the chopper and didn't waste a second taking out the armed guys trying to harm Eduardo and those around him. As her brother, she knew Marco would do whatever it took to keep her safe; he'd come looking for her.

The door cracked open, interrupting Suzie's thoughts. When she saw Sergio walk into the room, she couldn't help but roll her eyes in annoyance. He sat in front of her, his icy dark eyes piercing into her skull. She stared back at him.

"Let's cut the bullshit," said Sergio. "So, you're Suzie, the

Grade 6 teacher/psychotherapist from Toronto, right? John Hegland, your partner, is highly regarded as the chief of staff at Toronto's largest community hospital, known for his exceptional surgical skills. Having attended high school with Eduardo, he feels a strong sense of responsibility to watch out for him. Marco, your brother, who used to be a radical in the FARC, has now transformed into a peaceful individual and works as a simple auto mechanic. Did I get it all right?"

Suzie continued to stare at him, not saying a word, as his diatribe didn't miss a beat. "The Rattazzi family's influence extends to approximately five per cent of Italy's gross domestic product," said Sergio, "giving them significant control over the country's economy. Eduardo's lack of stability and overall unsuitability make him unfit to assume the role of leading such a large company. The risks to Italy are too great, posing a significant threat to its stability. This could all end if you convince him to step down and transfer control to a family member of our choosing, someone who is better equipped to handle the responsibility."

Suzie knew his icy stare was an attempt to intimidate her. She smiled as she responded to Sergio with two loud words: "Fuck you!"

"Look," said Sergio. "You have seen the extent of our reach. We will eventually get to him. It could all stop now. It's up to you.

We are going to let you go now so you can think about things. John… Well, he may not get so lucky. What happens to him will depend on you and Eduardo." Sergio got up and left the room, the sound of the door slamming echoing through the room.

Suzie, consumed by anger, felt her heart pounding as adrenaline surged through her veins. She got up from the table and paced around the room, her footsteps echoing. The threats made about a loved one's safety carried a heavy weight. Sergio was determined to carry out his plan, which was to end Eduardo's life, just as he had intended all along. Convincing Eduardo to change his beliefs would have no impact on that mission whatsoever. Sergio was a cold-blooded killer. She could see that in his eyes.

The door opened and Suzie turned around. Luigi entered the room. He smiled at her. "You are free to go," he said.

"What, so you can follow me to Eduardo?" she retorted. "It is not going to work like that." Suzie angrily stormed out of the interrogation room, swiftly grabbing her cell phone and other belongings from the registration desk as she left the precinct. In the peaceful park located on the other side of the street, she found a comfortable spot on the bench and settled herself down. She knew Marco would come looking for her. She would wait patiently until he arrived.

As the sun began to rise, its early morning light slowly

filtered through the darkness, casting a gentle glow that reflected off the leaves of the trees. Suzie reflected upon her exhaustion, realizing just how tired she truly was. It had been over 24 hours since she had slept. Resting on the hard bench, she positioned herself on her side and, in a matter of 30 seconds, slipped into a deep slumber.

Chapter Thirty-Three

Marco and Eduardo took the front seats of the car, leaving Flavia and with her dog Angus to sit in the back. Flavia could see Suzie lying peacefully lying on the park bench, oblivious to their watchful gaze, as the soft breeze danced through the trees. The sounds of footsteps and panting dogs filled the air, but Suzie seemed completely unaware of the joggers and dog owners passing her by on that quiet morning. Silently exiting the car, Flavia leashed Angus and strolled along the sidewalk towards the park. As she stopped in front of the bench where Suzie was, Angus crouched behind and relieved himself on the grass. Bending over to pick up the excrement in a green plastic bag with her left hand, she gently slipped a note into the front pocket of Suzie's jeans.

"I'm Flavia, Eduardo's friend," she whispered to Suzie as she stirred awake. Flavia continued to concentrate her gaze on the grass. "I left a note in your front pocket. Follow the instructions. We'll see you there."

Out of the corner of her eye, Flavia could see Suzie stir and then watch her put the bag into the garbage bin. She seamlessly blended in with the other early morning crowd as she strolled down the street. Flavia thought back to the last time she'd seen Sergio Leone, who was then using the name Guido Massone. She knew he was the same person who was trying to kill Eduardo, but if he were watching her now, she doubted he would recognize the lanky and uncertain 17-year-old girl who had blossomed into a graceful and self-assured woman.

She had first met Guido at a coffee bar on her way to classes at the University of Turin 30 years ago. When she'd walked in that day, he had been sitting alone reading a newspaper in front of the espresso bar.

"That will be one euro," said the tall barista as she ordered. She could sense the stranger's penetrating stare as he glanced up from what he was reading. Flavia passed her Visa to the barista. He placed her card in the electronic credit card machine. It made a strange sound. He looked up at Flavia. "It rejected your card. I'll try again."

Flavia, perplexed, glanced at the machine. "It's a brand-new card. I used it here yesterday and there were no problems."

The barista shook his head. "Sorry, it's still not working. Do you have another way of paying?"

"I got it," said the handsome stranger, standing up and placing two euros on the counter. "These new machines are often more trouble than they are worth. I prefer good old-fashioned cash. Everyone takes cash."

Flavia felt her heart skip a beat when he turned to face her, captivated by his intense gaze. She stared back. His piercing dark eyes softened as they stood silently looking at each other. He touched her hand, gently lifted it to his lips, and kissed it. Flavia's pulse raced. Experiencing a wave of faintness, she didn't resist as he led her to a table and introduced himself.

They sat and talked for four hours, causing her to miss her political science class. Every intricate detail of her life seemed to hold a great fascination for him. In the past, no one had ever bothered to give her such undivided attention. During one conversation, Guido had seemed particularly interested in her father, Achille Grandi, who was a member of the communist party and leader of the automobile union. Just 17, Flavia had no interest in politics, but Guido had seemed to know many things about her father.

"Your father is a hero for the autoworkers," said Guido, during one particular conversation. "There is talk of a strike at the Fiat factory. All they are asking for is a decent wage. Did you know that the Rattazzi family has not given them a wage increase although inflation has raised costs by 20 per cent? Workers cannot afford to buy food!"

Flavia smiled. It was common knowledge that many regarded her father highly, yet hearing it from an intriguing and captivating stranger filled her with immense pride. The moment he'd extended the invitation for her to join him at his apartment for lunch that same day, she felt an overwhelming sense of euphoria, as if she were walking on clouds. For the following week, they spent most of their time in bed, passionately discovering one another's bodies. Given how much he admired her father, it was only a natural progression for her to invite Guido to her parents' house to meet him.

The dinner had been a great success. Her mother, an amazing cook who made the best veal parmesan in Turin, served her speciality that night. Guido and her father had engaged in a lengthy conversation about the current state of politics and the rampant issue of government corruption, the topic of discussion revolving around the expansive influence held by the Rattazzi family, as well as their exploitative treatment of the workers. Flavia and Guido hadn't left for his apartment until after midnight.

The next morning, as light streamed through the window, she'd woken up to the realization that she was the only one in the room. At 10 a.m., the phone rang, shattering the tranquility of the morning. She was told her father had peacefully passed away in his sleep. The coroner's preliminary examination pointed towards a heart attack as the cause of death.

Flavia now knew otherwise. Her previous beliefs about her lover had been shattered, leaving her feeling confused and betrayed.

Guido had slipped away like a ghost, leaving her with a lingering sense of loss. She was not only heartbroken, but six months after her father's death, the truth about Guido killing him became painfully clear. The weight of responsibility for having brought her father's murderer into her house still rested heavily on Flavia all these years later. Back then, when she'd filed a report accusing Guido of murder, the police had laughed at her with disbelief. She knew there would be no investigation since the police chief was Gianni Rattazzi's nephew.

When she'd approached the Rattazzi family about her concerns that they were involved with her father's death, they'd seemed genuinely shocked and upset. She'd met with the patriarch, Gianni and Marella, his wife—Eduardo's parents. Gianni had appeared hesitant, refusing to acknowledge any involvement in her father's death. With a heavy heart, Flavia had departed from that initial meeting, her hopes for accountability shattered.

It was a few weeks later when she'd received a phone call from Marella. "My heart is breaking for you," she'd told Flavia. "Too many things have happened, all for the sake of business. I cannot live like this. I want to help you. Let's meet again, just you and me."

Gradually, the two women became good friends. As the days turned into weeks, Flavia had found herself becoming Marella's confidante, their bond growing stronger amidst the web of deception surrounding her husband's business. Flavia was completely engrossed in the intricate family dynamics, as Marella manoeuvred through the tangled web of conflicting family loyalties in an attempt to maintain the unity of the family. As Eduardo grew up, Marella recognized he was different from the other boys who were chasing girls even before they hit puberty. His well-being weighed heavily on her, depriving her of sleep and leaving her both tired and anxious. With genuine concern for her friend, Flavia reached out to Eduardo, eager to understand him more deeply.

"Your mother and father don't want to accept that you're gay. They think I can convert you to a heterosexual," said Flavia as they sat on the veranda of her beach house on a deserted cove south of Cagliari in Sardinia. A warm summer breeze came from the Mediterranean as the sun was setting. The sky was a brilliant orange.

Eduardo sat in silence.

"Look," said Flavia, "if I hadn't agreed to it, they would have found someone else. I wouldn't want you to go through that," she continued. "I first met you when you were eight years old, and I knew then you were gay."

Eduardo looked at her incredulously. "How could you possibly know that?"

Flavia burst out in a laugh. "Look at me!" She stood up and

twirled. "Women like me constantly endure the objectifying gaze of men who undress us with their eyes. I can sense their thoughts, as if they were speaking directly to me. The way you gaze at me is unlike any look I've seen from a straight 17-year-old boy."

Eduardo seemed to become more relaxed. "You are truly a beautiful woman. I can understand why men desire you. Why is it you live alone, then?"

Flavia went silent and thought about her words. "A while ago, a man who I loved deeply scarred me. I am still recovering."

"What happened?"

"Maybe one day I'll tell you. Until then, let's be friends. We can tell your parents that things are going well with us, and you can come by and stay with me anytime you like. That way, they'll leave you alone, thinking I have 'cured' you," she said, gesturing at the absurdity of the term. "They never have to know the truth about us."

"Why would you do that for me?"

Flavia looked at him deeply. "You are a kind and sensitive person. One day, you will do great things. If I can help you along your way, that is all I need."

Eduardo stood up and gave Flavia a hug. Tears were in his eyes. "Thank you," was all he said.

As Flavia arrived at the restaurant and walked in with Angus on a leash, she spotted Marco and Eduardo. They were drinking their coffee when she sat down. Eduardo rubbed Angus' head as he tried to lick his hand. The dog wagged his stubby tail with happiness as Eduardo continued to rub behind his ears.

"I will never get over what that man did to my father," said Flavia. "Now he's trying to do the same thing to you, Eduardo. This must end now."

Before Eduardo or Marco could answer, Suzie walked into the restaurant.

Chapter Thirty-Four

The sudden explosion sent John flying off the bench, disoriented and alarmed. He was lying on the dusty floor, completely covered in a thick layer of dust. The noise from the loud blast left his ears ringing. When the explosion occurred, John was in a deep sleep, and it took him a moment to comprehend his surroundings in the jail cell. He glanced around the room. The other prisoners were waking up and seemed to be just as disoriented as he was. The obese man with the loud snores and the swollen face continued to sleep as if nothing had happened, although he was now on the floor, now covered with dust. Eyeing the hole in the wall, John recognized this might be an opportunity to get out. He immediately stood up as Marco burst in through the opening caused by the explosion.

"John, are you OK?" asked Marco as he grabbed him by the arm. "Let's go!"

John shook the dust off himself and took a last glance around the cell. None of his other cellmates had made a move. It seemed as though he was the only one who wanted to get out. John followed Marco.

After crawling out of the hole, the pair sprinted onto the road. A crowd had congregated on the street, their murmurs and gasps filling the air as they stared intently at an object or event beyond the precinct. From a distance of 100 metres, John could see flames engulfing a car, dancing, and reaching a height of 20 feet above it. Thick black smoke enveloped the wreckage, filling the air with an acrid smell. Marco's yell reverberated in the air, the excitement evident in his voice as he exclaimed, "We created a diversion!"

People were darting in every direction. A fire truck's siren filled the air, reverberating off the pavement with increasing volume as it drew closer to the scene. John and Marco dashed through the park, their feet pounding against the pavement until they reached a beat-up 1980s-era Toyota Corolla. The engine was already running, filling the air with the scent of exhaust while Flavia, Suzie, and Eduardo waited inside. John and Marco swiftly slipped through the open back door, pushing Angus onto the floor to make room.

Flavia drove to a storage facility on the outskirts of town, right next to a sandy beach. She was cautious and mindful of the speed limit, not wanting to attract any unwelcome notice. After inputting the security code, the gate to the complex swung open. Flavia pulled up to a storage unit with a door that rolled up and she used her key to unlock it. With a creak, the door slowly swung open, revealing a dimly lit room. After the others exited the car, Flavia backed it into the designated spot inside the storage room, then closed the door and locked it.

Angus eagerly headed towards the beach, diving into the

water with playful splashes. With a burst of energy, he effortlessly leaped into the dinghy that was secured to a mooring ball. Observing the actions of the others with his bashful eyes, he watched as they removed their shoes and socks, entered the water, and then positioned themselves comfortably on the rubber tubing of the inflatable dinghy. Flavia sat behind a small steering wheel and started the engine. With just one try, the 25-horsepower outboard engine roared to life. Marco untied the bowline from the mooring ball and Flavia set off, headed to her home on the private cove three miles away.

At the house on the beach, Marco sat with Flavia on the veranda, looking out on the cove; the others had gone to their rooms for a nap. The two sat on the wicker sofa in silence, comfortably swaddled by brightly coloured cushions. Only the break of small waves on the beach disrupted the quiet of their surroundings. After several minutes, Marco glanced at Flavia, catching her eye before speaking. "You know what you must do now," he said.

Flavia's eyes widened in astonishment. "How did you know?" she asked.

"To survive everything I have lived through," Marco explained, "I developed the ability to read people. Rarely am I incorrect. You and I are more alike than you could imagine. You're planning to kill Sergio, but you are uncertain how you'll do it. I am going to tell you."

Marco spent the next 30 minutes describing what he had in mind. Flavia listened intently, asking questions along the way. "Do you really think I can do this?" she asked.

He locked eyes with her, his gaze filled with unwavering conviction. "I have never been more certain of anything else in my life."

Flavia had a softness in her eyes as she reached out and caressed Marco's cheek with the back of her fingers. It was like electricity going through his body. Marco felt his heart skip a beat as she leaned over to kiss him. She smelled like fresh lilacs. She pushed her tongue into his mouth and held his head in her hands. Marco felt himself getting aroused. It had been many years since a woman had made him feel like this. Flavia suddenly disentangled herself from him, stood up, and grabbed his hand. "Follow me," she whispered. She led him into her bedroom and closed the door.

"I have waited for this moment for the last 30 years," said Flavia. The five of them sat around her kitchen table. Angus lay on the floor at Eduardo's feet with one eye open, looking up at him. The faint scent of freshly brewed coffee filled the air as they focused on their conversations and cemented their plan. "Let's go over it again."

"Have you got the stuff I suggested?" asked John.

"Marco picked up everything this morning, so I am ready and know what to do. He let me practice on him," said Flavia.

"I'll make the phone call," said Suzie. "We'll arrange to meet up with Sergio in the same restaurant we were at this morning. Marco will be already there as backup in case the shit hits the fan. John and I will stay here until it is safe."

"OK," said Eduardo, "Let's get started." He passed the phone to Suzie, who dialled and put the phone on speaker. Everyone was silent.

Sergio picked up on the first ring. They could all hear his soft breathing as he listened to what Suzie had to say. "Eduardo has given due consideration to your proposal," she said. "Although I advised against it, he is open to discussing this matter further with you. Running away has become exhausting for him and he is tired of it. He longs for a time when he was unnoticed and nobody showed any interest in him, wishing for things to return to the way they were. Despite the challenges, Eduardo is eager to arrange a meeting with you. It must be with you only and no one else. At Trattoria Timonte Ristorante. Be there at 3 p.m. He will bring his friend, Flavia, so don't try anything." Suzie paused, waiting for a response.

Without saying a word, Sergio disconnected the phone.

"That is as close to a confirmation as we'll get, I suppose," said Suzie. "Marco, why don't you head over there now and make sure he doesn't bring reinforcements? Eduardo and Flavia, you'll leave in three hours."

Marco got up from the table and headed to the beach shed that concealed *Allegro*'s dinghy. "I'll give you a hand pushing off," said John as he walked with Marco. When they were close to the shed, John asked, "Marco, why are you doing all this, risking your life and taking chances when you could be safe at home in Toronto, watching Netflix?"

Marco stopped in his tracks. "John, your exceptional surgical abilities and your unwavering support for my sister make you her ideal partner. She loves you and would follow blindly to keep you safe. It's obvious to me that dealing with someone like Sergio is not your strong suit. In the blink of an eye, he would annihilate you as effortlessly as crushing a bug under his foot. You are like family to me, and I feel a deep sense of responsibility to keep you safe. Besides, I never watch Netflix."

John and Marco strained as they hauled the dinghy out of the shed and launched it into the water. John watched as Marco jumped in and made his way to the stern. With a gentle splash, he lowered the engine into the water and gave the cord a firm tug to start it. It took two pulls, but finally it sputtered to life, the engine humming with a slight vibration. Marco backed the dinghy into deeper water before turning around, the sound of the engine echoing across the open ocean. With a casual wave of his hand, he revved the engine, and the roar of the motor filled the air as he sped towards Cagliari, the sound gradually fading as he disappeared down the bay. John couldn't help but reflect on his good fortune to have such a vigilant guardian angel.

Chapter Thirty-Five

Marco sat in a dark corner of the trattoria, hidden away from the flickering candlelight and chatter of other patrons. The table was in the shadows created by a wall of wine bottles. He could clearly see between the racks and hear everything that was said in the restaurant from his concealed position. Most patrons had left after the lunch rush. Although open all day, the bustling activity at the restaurant peaked at night as families seeking authentic Italian cuisine drifted in. It was nearly 3 p.m. A tired-looking family of three small children and their exhausted parents were the only others in the restaurant. The kids ran around, their laughter echoing through the air, while the parents sipped their red wine.

Marco saw the restaurant door open. Eduardo and Flavia entered, sitting down at a table near the door. The long-haired male server with a sleeve tattoo running up his left arm approached with menus and asked if he could bring them drinks right away. From the shadows at the rear of the restaurant, Marco watched as the server wrote on a notepad and then walked away. A few minutes later, he appeared with their drinks. Marco glanced at his watch. It was 3:12 p.m. *Maybe Sergio won't turn up.*

As Marco kept his eyes trained on the restaurant door, he could hear the thundering footsteps of the three children racing past him. He glanced over just as the oldest one abruptly halted, causing the child behind him to lose his balance and collide with the table's edge. The child emitted a loud howl, which echoed throughout the room. "Mommy, mommy," he screamed and ran toward his parents. The other two children who had been causing chaos finally stopped their rampage and joined their parents, where their mother was comforting their crying sibling.

"We want to go to the beach," whined one child.

The parents exchanged glances with one another, their eyes lingering on the half-finished bottle of wine sitting on the table. "We'll leave in just 30 minutes," the father firmly said.

"We want to go now! We wanted to go now," the three children chanted in unison.

Acknowledging defeat, the parents sighed, as if knowing it was time to cut their losses. They gathered their belongings, settled their bill, and leisurely strolled out of the restaurant. The restaurant was eerily quiet, with only the faint sound of cutlery clinking against plates breaking the silence.

Marco pulled out his phone to call Suzie with an update. The door opened, and light flooded inside the trattoria as Sergio walked inside. Marco's senses heightened when he observed his expensive suit and the confident swagger, signalling his belief that he had complete control—or was great at bluffing. He took a seat directly across from Eduardo and Flavia, positioning himself to have a clear view of both.

"It's been a long time," said Eduardo.

Sergio stared at Eduardo, saying nothing. After 10 long seconds of silence, he spoke, his eyes icy. "You have something to say to me?"

Before Eduardo could reply, the tattooed server came to the table and asked, "What can I get you?"

"I'll have a Pernod on ice," said Sergio. His gaze remained fixated on Eduardo, who was squirming in his seat.

"Why have you tried to kill me?" asked Eduardo.

"It's nothing personal," said Sergio. "Our acquaintance dates back to your childhood, so I have known you for quite some time. The crux of the matter lies in our organization's lack of confidence that can effectively handle the operations of the Rattazzi business. The Brothers of Italy do not want a drug-addicted camel jockey who sympathizes with Muslim terrorists to lead Europe's largest company. It should be clear to you by now that we have no intention of allowing that. That position is not attainable for you under any circumstances. I will go as far as taking your life if necessary. I'm hoping we can find an alternative solution that satisfies both of our desires."

Eduardo stared at Sergio, straightening up and leaning

forward. Marco knew it had been several years since Eduardo had last felt in charge of his own future, but now he could see in Eduardo's eyes that he'd regained a sense of control. Sergio glanced over at Flavia just as the server returned with the Pernod and placed it in front of him.

"You don't remember me, do you?" asked Flavia. "You went by Guido Massone when we first met."

Marco could see Sergio pale when the recognition from 30 years ago flooded back to him. His eyes darted around from Eduardo, then to Flavia. "What is this?" he shouted. Without warning, Eduardo rose from his seat, hitting the edge of the table forcibly. The Pernod spilled across Sergio's lap. In a sudden surge of panic, he shot up from his seat and wiped the spilled drink off his pants with his hands, looking down at his soiled suit. In that split second, Flavia sprung up and swiftly injected a syringe into his neck, releasing the contents directly into his jugular vein.

Sergio swatted at his neck, knocking the now empty syringe across the room towards Marco. Confusion spread across Sergio's face as he looked up from Flavia, then back to Eduardo. He slumped back into his seat and his eyes stopped moving, looking straight ahead. Marco quietly got up from his chair and retrieved the syringe from the floor. He removed the needle, sticking it into the soft wood under the tabletop to hide it and placed the harmless, empty syringe in his pocket.

"I just injected you with 150 milligrams of succinylcholine," said Flavia, looking at the man who'd betrayed her decades ago. "It's a paralyzing agent. You can hear me, but you cannot move or breathe."

Hidden in the shadows of the restaurant, Marco's vantage point allowed him to witness the telltale fasciculations of small muscles as the drug started to have an impact on Sergio, who sat completely still. Eduardo fixed his intense gaze on the man who had been relentlessly pursuing him.

Flavia continued to talk. "You deceived me, making me believe you were in love with me, only to manipulate me into getting close to my father and ending his life. Not only did you break my heart, but the weight from the guilt of bringing you into my home to kill my father has burdened me my entire life. Since then, I have found it difficult to place my trust in any man. You ruined everything; my entire world crumbled," she said, raising her voice slightly. Flavia leaned back, letting a smile come to her lips. "You have three minutes left to live. Before you die, I will be the last person you lay your eyes on. This is the moment I've been waiting for the last 30 years."

Eduardo and Flavia watched silently as Sergio's vacant stare became glassy. Flavia leaned over the table and felt for his carotid pulse. There was none. She held up a finger, nodding at Marco, and waited a minute longer before calling the server.

"There is something wrong with this man," she said when the server arrived.

With a perplexed look on his face, the server gently pushed on Sergio's shoulder. His body leaned over to the left. The server grabbed his shirt and pulled him upright. The server went pale. "Oh, my God!" he cried. "He is not breathing! Help! Help! Quick! Someone call an ambulance." With the shirt slipping from the server's hands, Sergio tumbled down to the floor.

The cook ran from the kitchen in his white apron. "I know CPR!" he cried out. He began cardiac massage. "Quick! Get the defibrillator." He pointed to a red box that was on the wall near the entrance to the washrooms.

The server sprinted to the defibrillator. Marco watched him pause to read the directions, then rushed to where Sergio lay. "The instructions explicitly stated to place pads on the patient's chest and then administer the defibrillator," he shouted as he pressed the adhesive pads onto Sergio, ensuring they stuck firmly in place.

The cook shouted while looking at the monitor. "He has asystole. The AED will not defibrillate." He continued the CPR until the ambulance arrived two minutes later. With the EKG leads in place, the paramedics exchanged worried glances as they confirmed the absence of all electrical activity from the heart. They declared Sergio dead. With a shake of his head, the paramedic informed them, "You can discontinue the CPR."

Marco observed the entire scene from his table at the rear of the restaurant, going unnoticed amid all the chaos. Flavia had moved away from the group, positioning herself near the door, her eyes scanning the room with a hint of apprehension. Her face remained blank as she watched, seemingly captivated by the desperate efforts to resuscitate her former lover. His mouth agape, Eduardo's eyes flitted nervously between the cook, the server, and Sergio.

The paramedics gently lifted Sergio onto the gurney, ensuring they fully covered his body with the orange blanket. Taking great care, they slowly manoeuvred the gurney towards the ambulance. Just outside the restaurant door, one paramedic engaged in conversation with a police officer, who was shaking his head with a disappointed expression. The uniformed cop walked into the restaurant and approached Flavia.

"Can you tell us what happened?"

"I have no idea. I don't know who he is," said Flavia. "I was having a Diet Coke with my friend when that man sat down with us. He said he didn't feel well—that his blood sugar was low. He asked if we could buy him a Pernod. Then he fell over. That's when the server came over and called out for help."

After writing Flavia's statement on a notepad, the police officer directed a glance at Eduardo, who was sitting at the table. "I do not know who he is either or why he didn't just speak to the server directly," said Eduardo. He shook his head. "I'm sorry. He must have had a heart attack or something."

The police officer glanced around the room. Seeing no one else to interview, he then asked for their names and contact info, writing them in his notebook. The police officer walked out the door to the ambulance and spoke with the paramedic. After a brief conversation, both returned to their vehicles and drove away.

Marco, satisfied that everything was under control, discreetly slipped out of the restaurant through the back exit.

Chapter Thirty-Six

"What do you think will become of Eduardo?" asked Suzie.

John and Suzie sat in the economy section of Alitalia Airlines. They were on a direct flight from Rome to Toronto and would arrive in six hours.

"I think his future is a lot more secure with Marco agreeing to stay with him for the next month," replied John.

"Eduardo places more trust and confidence in Marco than he does in his own security staff. My brother always looked after me. Once his protective instincts kick in, he becomes an unstoppable force, willing to overcome any obstacle in his path. We witnessed him at his finest during this fiasco of a trip."

"Doesn't it worry you that your brother is… well… so violent?"

Suzie looked at John incredulously. "You are so lucky to have grown up in a civilized world, sheltered from the realities of what humans will do to one another. Your refined manners and articulate conversations would undoubtedly expose you to a premature death in Colombia. To survive in my world, you not only need to size up a threat within a fraction of a second, but you must eliminate the threat before you have had time to think about it. Marco can do that. I can do that. But you cannot. You would probably ponder whether it is a genuine threat. You would take a moment to reflect and ask yourself if you might be overreacting. Knowing you so well, I am certain you would conclude that you had overreacted. Besides, you do not know how to disable or eliminate a threat. In the 10 seconds it took you to think things through, you would be dead."

John sighed. This trip had been a harsh wake up call for him, forcing him to confront the realities of the world. Immersed in a career of saving lives for the last 10 years, he was now faced with the stark contrast of an alternative world where extinguishing life is effortless, like turning off a light switch.

"Where do you think Eduardo sits on this spectrum in dealing with threats?" John asked. "Is he more like you and Marco, walking around like spring-loaded weapons, or is he closer to me, naïve and innocent?"

"Eduardo is naïve and innocent, much more so than you. Despite your fear of heights, he trusted you to safely guide him down the mountain, which was significant after the first attempt on his life. You could have just as easily ended his life by falling into a crevasse with him in tow. Even though they only met a week ago, he feels a strong sense of trust towards Marco. And what's with his shift to Shia Muslim? Is he going to convert back to Catholicism now that he's running the largest business group in Europe? I hope he has honest and reliable business partners to guide him." Suzie shook her head.

"Not only is Eduardo highly intelligent," said John, "but he also shows great care and concern for others. It was evident in his interactions with Flavia that he cares deeply for her. He holds a deep and sincere affection for her. His care for us is evident in the way he always tried to help and protect us. He cared about Peter and acted as an anesthesiologist, even when he was clearly out of his comfort zone. Don't you think he'll soldier through and be able to do the right thing for the company? So many depend on him. He's sensitive and empathetic."

"I fear others will mislead him into trouble. I know he is your friend, and you might not want to hear this, but his trust in others will lead to his downfall."

John thought about this. He was the same way. Many times he'd trusted others, even when there was no solid foundation for such faith. He knew this was a weakness in his character, but he had Suzie to steer him clear and guide him. She had prevented him from getting into trouble more times than he could remember.

John found comfort in the cushioned headrest as he gently laid his head down and closed his tired eyes. Suzie had put on her headphones and was engrossed in watching a movie. Despite feeling tired, he knew that the full impact of everything he had experienced had not yet caught up with him. Suzie's self-defence attack on Antonia with the gaff had left his school friend with severe disabilities. *Why would he try to hurt us? There must be more to the story.*

John slowly drifted off, and as sleep took over, vivid images filled his mind. In his dream, he was back in high school. He and Antonio could hear the roaring waves crashing against the sides of the racing dinghy off the coast of South Wales, feeling the thrill of danger as indestructible teenagers. They were laughing as the sailboat took them up and down the waves, splashing them with the frigid Bristol channel water. The wetsuits kept them warm. An especially enormous wave crashed into the boat, forcing Antonio to lose his grip on the tiller. The sailing dinghy capsized but righted itself in a few seconds. A wave swept overboard Antonio. But with a few swift moves, he crawled back into the boat. When Antonio turned around, John saw the sharp hook of a gaff lodged in Antonio's eye. John could hear himself screaming.

"Wake up, wake up," cried Suzie. "You are having a bad dream. It's OK honey." John could feel his shoulders moving as Suzie vigorously shook him out of his slumber. He was hyperventilating and sweat covered his brow, although it was cold on the plane. His head swivelled left, then right, before his gaze fixated on Suzie. He could see the lines of worry on her face.

"I think I'm OK now," he whispered. "It was a bad dream. It was Antonio. I saw him with the gaff in his eye."

John became quiet before asking Suzie, "Why do you think he tried to harm us? We were such good friends at school."

"I don't think it was you he was trying to harm. It was Eduardo. Regrettably, you were an unintended bystander. I believe you didn't know him at all. When I initially met him two years ago, you had no clue that he was trying to make advances towards me. To begin with, there is certainly a loose wire in his mind. Greed is the driving force for individuals like that. Although the reasons remain unknown, Eduardo's presence posed a menacing threat to his way of life."

"I'm going to make a prediction," said John. "Eduardo will surprise us. I believe in his kind-heartedness and his determination to always give his best effort. As his empire expands, we can look forward to hearing more about his thoughtful actions to ease pain and suffering among those he works with, leaving a positive impact on the world."

Letting out a heavy sigh, Suzie settled back into her seat, headphones on, as she resumed watching her movie. In just two hours, the plane would touch down in Toronto. John fell into a deep, dreamless sleep, oblivious to the world around him.

Chapter Thirty-Seven

Eduardo anxiously awaited the meeting with Ayatollah Khamenei in his Tehran headquarters. He glanced at his watch and could feel the weight of time passing. The minutes turned into hours, and he continued to wait. Political tensions rising between the two countries led to the cancellation of all direct flights from Italy to there. After being re-routed to Abu Dhabi, the flight to Tehran ended up taking a total of 18 hours. Over the course of the past six months, Eduardo had embarked on this journey four times, always staying for a week. He split his time between attending mosque and holding meetings with Iranian government officials.

"There you are, my good friend," said the booming voice of the Ayatollah.

Eduardo stood up so they could embrace. "It is great to see you with all that is going on right now," said Eduardo.

"Come. Come have some tea," said the Ayatollah.

They sat together on floor cushions surrounding a small table. A server brought some tea and poured it into gold-leafed small cups. They drank.

"What is going on?" asked Eduardo.

The Ayatollah sighed before he spoke. "All we want is to live peacefully. That is what the Quran is all about. Not everyone in the world understands that. We—"

The call to prayer coming from a muezzin and loudspeaker interrupted the conversation. The Ayatollah and Eduardo unrolled the mats set in the corner specifically for prayers and faced east. They recited the *adhan* together: *Allahu akbar, Allahu akbar* (Allah is the greatest, Allah is the greatest) … After 10 minutes, when they had finished their prayers, they rolled up their mats and returned to the table.

Eduardo glanced at the Ayatollah again. "I read the Quran from cover to cover again last week. It talks about peace and living together with our neighbours in harmony. Why are Hezbollah, our brothers in Lebanon, attacking Israel? They don't read the Quran?"

"To attain peace, we need to eliminate the infidels who attack us for no reason."

"That's not what the Quran says."

"Look, we are all grateful for the funding you have funnelled to us for the Muslim cause. It is because of you that no one will attack us for fear of nuclear retaliation; we have the biggest arsenal in the region."

Eduardo went white. "You… you said the money would go to help fellow Muslims to live in peace. What's this about a nuclear arsenal?"

The Ayatollah smiled. "We have the right to defend ourselves against the infidels; otherwise, they will wipe us out. That will never happen now. We sent our first nuclear missile to America. Washington, DC, should be a nuclear wasteland in..." The Ayatollah glanced at his watch "...15 minutes from now."

"What...what's the matter with you? That's not what I agreed to when I sent you all those billions. You said it would improve the lives of the impoverished Muslims from the sanctions America had levied for all those years. You lied to me. Oh, my God. What have I done?"

The Ayatollah went red in the face. "You call me a liar," he said, his voice filled with indignation. "I can't believe you would have the audacity to do that. You are asserting yourself as someone who is superior and arrogant. Your behaviour is disgusting and nothing more than what I would expect from a junkie and faggot." Spittle escaped from his lips as he yelled and became more agitated. "Have you ever wondered about the perspective of the Quran regarding homosexuality? Faggots receive the punishment of being stoned to death. The only reason I haven't ordered that for you is because of all the money you have given us." He glared at Eduardo.

Eduardo couldn't believe what he was hearing coming from the leader of the Muslim world. This could not be happening. *The Ayatollah was no different from the Brothers of Italy and other political leaders. What happened to the brotherly love and peace that he'd promised? Now he's sent a nuclear warhead to America? This will be the end of the world as we know it. I have failed.*

The cell phone inside the Ayatollah's cloak rang. He looked at the number and smiled. "Ahh. It's my top general calling to give me the good news. We've annihilated the infidels of America!" He answered the call.

Eduardo watched as his face turned from all smiles to one of horror. "You incompetent fool!" he shouted.

The Ayatollah ended the call abruptly, his hurried footsteps echoing as he raced out of the room, leaving Eduardo alone. Suddenly, the blaring sound of air raid sirens bombarded his ears. Eduardo got up and looked out of the window, observing the panic of people scattering in various directions on the bustling street below. On the horizon, a massive orange cloud billowed into the sky. Not understanding what was happening, Eduardo stared at the brightness for a few seconds. The building shook slightly at first, and then the floor beneath him crumbled. As he felt his body get lifted to the sky, Eduardo had one last thought. *What have I done?*

Then blackness.

Chapter Thirty-Eight

Returning to the safety of Toronto felt like a warm embrace. It had been six months since John had resumed his surgical practice, and during this time, he had settled comfortably into his routine. His role as chief of staff took up a substantial amount of his time, but he often thought about Eduardo. Driving home in his SUV, a smile came to his face as he remembered his friend belting out opera from the medivac sled as they traversed the treacherous crevasses of the Khumbu Icefall while he battled his fear of heights. Eduardo trusted him. And John was worried about Eduardo's innocence and trusting nature. Unscrupulous predators would find it too tempting not to take advantage of him. His cell phone chirped from its holder to the right of the steering wheel. John put it on hands free.

"When are you coming home?" asked Suzie.

"I'm in the Honda right now," said John. "Should I pick up some Chinese takeout on my way home?"

"No. I have your favourite for tonight. Linguini. Maybe grab a bottle of red. It's our third year together… Don't tell me you forgot?"

"Errr…" John hesitated. "Yep, you caught me. I forgot." They both laughed. "Will do."

John stopped at the wine store, quickly choosing a bottle of

Châteauneuf-du-Pape. They were celebrating, so a nice bottle of red wine was appropriate. Minutes later, he walked into their house to the aroma of pasta cooking.

Suzie was sitting in the living room watching TV. She glanced up at him. Something wasn't right.

"There's been a nuclear explosion in Iran," said Suzie. "Tehran has suffered utter devastation, with the city being levelled and transformed into a nuclear wasteland." She paused, not taking her eyes off the screen. "They said the explosion killed more than 10 million people."

John sat on the sofa next to Suzie. It was a special newscast on the CBC. Every station had interrupted its regular programming to report on the devastating story. Drone views of the city in rubble filled the screen. There were bodies lying everywhere, some blackened by the explosion. Not a single building remained as far as the horizon. Small fires burned, but there was a large one on the right of the screen, the flames reaching into the sky. John and Suzie silently looked at the destruction. A blond news reporter appeared on-screen.

"The destruction is from a nuclear explosion in Iran," she explained. "The details are sketchy, but the blast was from a targeted missile launched by the United States. Let's go to the spokesperson for the department of defence."

The image of a sombre-faced, middle-aged man filled the screen. "At 0112 this morning, the Aegis Ballistic Missile Defense System destroyed a nuclear warhead over the Arctic launched from a base near Tehran, Iran. The intended target was Washington, DC. The Israel Defence Force simultaneously destroyed a missile against Israel in mid-air. In retaliation, the United States launched a non-nuclear strike against Iran using drone technology from our aircraft carrier in the Mediterranean, the USS *Gerald R. Ford*. The strike triggered a chain reaction from the nuclear arsenal storage base near Tehran. It was their own nuclear weapons that resulted in the massive destruction you've seen from the drone images."

John and Suzie looked at each other in shock, then fixated their eyes on the fallout caused by the explosion. The blond news reporter was back. "The information coming from the Stockholm International Peace Research Institute claims that Iran secretly acquired nuclear weapons over the past six months. They stored them, unbeknownst to the international community, in a base near Tehran. The drone strike triggered a series of nuclear explosions and destroyed everything within a 50-mile radius."

The image on the screen showed the words News Alert. It cut to a white-haired man with the name S. Mattarella, President of Italy below. He was speaking in Italian, but simultaneous English translation appeared in the captions. "We are searching for Eduardo Rattazzi, who we suspect of funnelling billions of dollars to Iran from the empire he inherited six months ago for the purpose of acquiring the nuclear arsenal. A picture of Eduardo appeared."

Suzie and John looked at each other in horror. "Oh, my God!" whispered Suzie. "This is terrible!" They turned their attention back to the television newscast.

"We are also searching for a sleeper cell of highly trained terrorists…"

The pictures of John, Suzie, and Marco appeared on the screen.

The End